Seahorse

Seahorse

graham petrie

SOHO

First published in Great Britain by
Constable and Company Limited in 1980

Published by
Soho Press, Inc.
853 Broadway
New York, NY 10003

Library of Congress Cataloging-in-Publication Data

Petrie, Graham.
Seahorse/Graham Petrie.
p. cm.
ISBN 1-56947-077-4
(acid-free paper)
I. Title.
PR9199.3.P453S4 1996
813'.54—dc20   95-8673
                                  CIP

Manufactured in the United States
10 9 8 7 6 5 4 3 2 1

For Anne

Seahorse

'Tell me about Dr Daniels.'

A brief flash of the teeth, curiously pointed. A shake of the head. The shoulder-length grey hair sways, undulates, falls immaculately back into place, not a strand awry. I thought at first that they were wigs, those elaborate coiffures, they all wear them, men, women, children, but I have stroked them, even tugged them, and they hold firm to the skull.

'Scientist?' I repeat the word slowly. 'Is that what you said?'

A nod this time. Another mumbled word: 'evolwers'.

Again I repeat: 'Revolvers? Guns? Weapons? You want to attack the Institute?'

A nod, then a shake of the head. I have been among them long enough to know that sometimes, unpredictably, or perhaps following some pattern to which I have not yet seized the key, they reverse the order of information: cause follows effect, answer precedes question, time is jumbled, fragmented, deconstructed. This is one of these occasions: patiently I disentangle, recompose, construct. Yes, they want to attack the Institute; no, he does not mean revolvers.

I puzzle it out, but arrive nowhere. Finally he loses patience, drops to all fours, scampers grotesquely about, points his muzzle to an imaginary moon, howls, bares those yellow teeth which, I now see, are sharpened, as though with a file.

'Werewolf?' He nods. 'You think there are werewolves at the Institute?' And not only that, he confirms, but vampires too. He mimes a bat, fluttering over the grey, white-capped stretch of water that separates the mainland from the island, barely visible at the moment through the fog. He confides in me: 'They eat our souls,' he whispers.

I restrain myself from laughing, but he recognises the twitch in my cheek. The badly-suppressed rictus offends him and he moves away, accompanied by his companions. Seen from the back, with their grey hair and their identical black suits, shiny with years of wear, they are indistinguishable. I wonder if I will recognise him when we meet again.

Dreams, someone else informs me, the Institute is a Factory for Dreams. Nightmares are manufactured there, are tested on the defenceless villagers as they sleep. No one, I was solemnly assured, had ever dreamt in the village before Daniels and his companions arrived; now their nights are made hideous by gibbering monsters squatting at the foot of their beds, leering at them. From there they leap to the pillow to whisper lurid incitements to rape, violence, murder. Virgins dream of intercourse and awake deflowered. Ancient crones are intercepted staggering to the beds of teenage grandsons. Husbands awake in an empty bed and from the kitchen hear the sound of metal scraping against stone, the cautious whetting of a carving knife.

'Absurd,' I murmured. I was standing on the beach, staring across the bay at the headland on which the Institute is built, a massive stone building from at least the fifteenth century with – naturally – an evil reputation. It is inaccessible from three sides, the cliff falling sheer away from its surrounding walls; it can be reached only by a narrow pathway, blocked by an iron gate. After the previous night's storm, the sea was calm, the sky a brilliant blue, the sun a flaming yellow ball.

My informant waited patiently by my side. Like all the villagers, he is much smaller than I, reaching barely to my shoulder. His face is heavily lined, though probably more from exposure to wind and sea than from age, for he appears fairly young. The lines are caked with dirt, the teeth uneven and badly cared-for. I thought at first that he was the man to whom I had spoken previously, and it was only after a series of misapprehensions and false assumptions on my part that he revealed that *he* was called Hanslett and the other (whom I briefly described – long, grey hair, black suit, wrinkled features, poor teeth, aged between twenty and forty) was undoubtedly Ellicott or Endicott (the scream of a gull intervened as he spoke the name and I failed to catch it properly), a character (he claimed) renowned for untrustworthiness and unreliability.

'Did he tell you about the nets?' he enquired. I detected a sneer in his voice.

'The nets?'

Endicott/Ellicott and his crew, he explained, believed that a man's soul left his body every night to wander, converse, disport itself with other souls while the body slumbered, regaining strength for the following day. The souls of this particular community (so E. & E. believed, though the enlightened Hanslett scorned such superstition) were accustomed to assemble on the deserted island about a mile from the shore that I could now see quite clearly, a flat, unprepossessing place, almost barren of trees and with what appeared to be the ruins of a tower or lighthouse in the extreme left-hand corner. Souls are particularly vulnerable during such excursions: if anything should damage them or impede their return to an awakening body, the results could be catastrophic.

'And? – ' I waited impatiently for the conclusion. The sun was almost at its peak by now and the heat intense. I was dressed far too warmly for the weather: yesterday I had shivered in the cold winds that drove inland from the mist-enshrouded sea and now, in my sweater and heavy trousers, I was almost fainting from the heat. I had been warned, though, not to remove any clothing, even the most innocuous, in the presence of the villagers, whose vestmental codes were obscure and unpredictable.

'Well? –' The sweat trickled from my forehead into the corner of my eye, and I rubbed it hastily away.

Well, Elli/Endicott claimed that, when returning late from fishing one evening, his boat having been blown off-course by a storm, he had passed a small motor boat heading towards the island. In it sat Dr Daniels, his mane of pure white hair streaming picturesquely in the breeze, the young woman who generally did the shopping for the Institute in the village, and two others. The only rational explanation for their presence, according to Erracott (was that, after all, the name?) was that they were attempting to interfere with the villagers' souls as they went about their legitimate nocturnal business.

'And *you* believe?' I prompted.

He shrugged. The consequence was, he continued, that Ellicott (clearly, at last, this was the name!) and his friends had taken to assembling on the beach each evening and arranging the fishermen's nets, as they hung out to dry, to form a continuous and impassable barrier about ten feet high all along that section of the shore facing the island. For the souls, though immaterial, had a mysterious tangibility of their own that would not allow them through the coarse-spun reticulations of the nets. Also, as they flew to the island at a height that barely skimmed the surface of the waves, soaring and descending like birds or mirthful bats, it stood to reason that a ten-foot high obstacle would easily deter them.

'And so the souls are forced to remain on the beach at night instead? Are they content with this arrangement?'

'Oh, souls . . .' he muttered, with a disdainful gesture of his right hand. 'Who believes that nonsense?'

So *his* soul did not participate in the nocturnal revels? Or could it, perhaps, take part without his knowledge or consent?

He turned on his heel, abruptly, and left me, without a word. I watched him for a moment, until the glare of the sun became too painful; his figure wavered and shimmered in the heat, it stretched, shrank, widened, and split into separate components like a distorted reflection from a funfair mirror. I squeezed my eyes shut and, when I opened them again, he had vanished. Gratefully I removed my pullover, my shirt, my undervest, and prepared to relax in the sun.

That evening my bedside telephone rang, or rather it grated and wheezed in pathetic parody of the full-blooded melody to which I am accustomed at home. Nothing works here as it should: the villagers, in what must have been a primary flush of enthusiasm, have assembled all the paraphernalia of mid-twentieth century civilisation – telephones, television, radios, refrigerators, washing machines, dishwashers, even a couple of computers – and have then complacently allowed them to rot and disintegrate unused. It seems clear, for one thing, that the range of high mountains that rises abruptly about five miles outside the village, effectively cutting it off from normal communication with the wider world, would also block all radio and television reception, and, when I asked Ellicott which programmes the villagers regularly watched or listened to, he stared at me in blank amazement. I have not yet been invited to enter any of the houses but, from my glimpses of the kitchen of the hotel in which I am living, it seems that the refrigerator is used mostly for storing documents and ledgers, while all washing, of clothes or dishes, is carried out (sometimes, it appears, simultaneously) by the landlord's wife. I try not to be too squeamish about these matters and, in fact, the lack of a refrigerator is scarcely noticeable, the unvarying menu for every meal being freshly caught fish or other seafood. Fortunately there is abundant variety of these and the landlord's wife, whatever her deficiencies where hygiene is concerned, cooks them to perfection, with elegant simplicity and the minimum of adornment.

I lifted the receiver. There was a long pause, broken only by the sound of heavy breathing. I recognised the landlord who, though perfectly fluent and articulate when speaking his own language, becomes alarmingly asthmatic when talking English, wheezing in a distressingly painful manner and stumbling into virtual incoherence by the end of every sentence. I have tried repeatedly to assure him that I speak his own language like a native, having spent many laborious months mastering it in preparation for my visit, but, from my first attempt onwards, he has blandly ignored this, trying out all the tongues to which his profession has allowed him a degree of access – French, Italian, German, Polish, Russian, Arabic – before settling for an infantile form of broken English. To my disgust, I find myself lapsing into this pidgin speech when talking to him, for I am perfectly aware that the calm smile on his face, the regular nodding of the head when I talk to him at my normal speed, signifies total incomprehension rather than the mutual understanding he intends to convey.

'Mr Everrich?' (his mangling of my name suggests an optimism about my financial prospects that I am far from sharing). 'You have speech with man from village?' The sentence trailed away into what might be either a question or a statement that had run out of breath.

'Yes,' I replied cautiously.

'He here now.' Another pause, while the receiver was handed to someone beside him: 'Mr Averridge?' (another mangling, but let it pass).

The new voice sounded familiar. 'Is that Ellicott?' I hazarded.

'Who?'

'Ellicott. I spoke to you yesterday.'

'No Ellicott here.' He did not, however, offer an alternative name, but went on to say that he had heard (from whom? from Hanslett?) that I was interested in watching the assembling of the nets that evening.

'To catch the souls?'

'Protect them. Not catch them. Who can catch a soul?'

He said that he was waiting in the lobby and I went down to join him. Despite his denial, I was certain that he was indeed Ellicott, and the glimpse of pointed teeth when he smiled at me in welcome confirmed this. He greeted me with a neutrality that might indicate either long acquaintance or a first, professional, encounter, and we set out together towards the beach.

We walked through the village square, where the glint of moonlight on the worn statuary of the fountain sent gleams of chill intelligence into the eyes of the figures as we passed. A crowd had already gathered on the beach, men and women in the customary black clothing, and even a scattering of children. Illumination was provided, partly by the moon and partly by torches soaked in pitch that were carried by about a third of the participants. Several of the nets had already been assembled: contrary to my expectations, they formed, not a single barrier stretching along the shore-line, but a much more complex structure, several layers deep, full of what appeared to be passages and entrance-ways.

Ellicott (I will call him that for convenience) explained that the souls would be bored, and perhaps even angered, by a mere confinement to the beach, which offered – he spread his right arm wide in a gesture of confirmation – little to inspire or entertain them. The villagers had therefore arranged the nets in the form of a maze or labyrinth, with multiple entrances on the landward side, a rendezvous at the centre but, of course, no exits towards the sea. The souls, in this manner, were afforded hours of innocent amusement to compensate for the loss of their accustomed diversions on the island; they returned to their bodies at dawn refreshed and stimulated and as a result, he, for one, now found himself far more lively and alert when carrying out his daytime business than he had ever known himself before.

'And what about your dreams?' I asked. 'Do they reflect the souls' activities?'

'Dreams? No one here has dreams.'

'But you know what they are, nevertheless?'

'Some unscrupulous people, attention-seekers, sensationalists, claim to have dreams. They lie.'

'But how could they *invent* dreams if no one knows what they are?'

'We know what they are. We have read books. Freud. We have read Freud. We know all the latest research. Rapid-eye-movements. We know all about that. Only we do not believe it.' He corrected himself. 'Other people may have dreams, that I cannot deny. We do not.'

He turned away from me, in an obvious gesture of dismissal, and began to talk to one of the men who was involved with erecting the nets. I began to wander down the beach, glancing idly at the activity taking place around me. I passed a group of young women engaged in stretching a net tautly between two poles; one stood on tiptoe to achieve this and, for a moment, the shapeless black garment that normally swathes the village females from head to toe, concealing whatever charms they might possess, fell aside to reveal the outlines of two firm, youthful breasts, thrusting proudly against the confines of an almost transparent white blouse. I stopped to watch, hoping perhaps that my evident interest would draw some answering sign of recognition; instead she slumped back on her heels, drew her cloak around her in a gesture almost of terror, turned her face away and began to whimper, like an animal. Her friends clustered round her, to console her, and several shook their fists at me threateningly. I retreated hastily, hardly even looking to see where I was going and, before I quite realised what I was doing, I found I had backed into one of the openings among the nets. Losing my head, I blundered about wildly for a few seconds, and this was enough to draw me further into the labyrinth, instead of securing my exit: the nets were now all around me, making it impossible for me even to distinguish the gap by which I had originally entered.

I paused, and attempted to pull myself together. Work had already been completed on the area in which I found myself trapped and most of the villagers had moved several yards along the beach: ghostly shapes flitted to and fro in the intermittent glare of the torches and a low murmur of voices merged with the constant surge of the sea against the shore. I wondered whether to call out for assistance, but my position appeared so ludicrous that I preferred to try to extricate myself as inconspicuously as possible. The more I wandered among the nets, however, searching for one of the many paths that must lead to an exit, the more I became entangled; finally I found myself in what must be the heart of the maze, the spot in which the souls were reputed to congregate.

I realised that the villagers had completed work for the night and were preparing to return home. They had formed a ceremonial procession some twenty yards further along the beach and were drawn up in columns of two, with the guttering torches throwing their shadows in grotesquely shifting patterns over the sand that was still flooded with the rays of the full moon. It occurred to me that I might be left there to drown, caught like a rat in a trap by the remorselessly encroaching tide and, abandoning my pride, I screamed aloud for assistance.

One of the figures detached himself from the column and moved over to the outer fringe of the nets, holding his torch high in his left hand. I recognised Ellicott and pleaded with him to help me escape.

'You safe there,' he reassured me. 'Tide already turned.'

I switched from English to the local tongue and explained that I could hardly be expected to spend the night there, out in the open. For one thing, I had changed that afternoon from my thick clothing into a flimsy shirt and light-weight trousers; I was already shivering in the chill wind that drove in from the sea and, to make matters worse, was steadily becoming drenched by the cold spray that was flung up by the waves and hovered some seconds in the air before inexorably selecting me as its target.

'Everything O.K.' Ellicott continued, maddeningly and

imperturbably persisting with his pidgin English. 'You spend the night there. Very comfortable. Talk with souls. Tell us their thoughts tomorrow.'

'Ellicott,' I pleaded, 'I can't stay here. I'll freeze to death. Look, I'm shivering already.'

'No Ellicott here,' he replied. 'Height of summer. You not freeze. Dawn in less than six hours.'

I felt that he was mocking me and I insisted once again that he release me, either by coming through the labyrinth to escort me out, or by lowering the nets that formed a barrier to my escape.

He shook his head. He too would be lost in the labyrinth, he explained. And, once raised, the nets could not, under any circumstances, be lowered before the next morning. 'You talk with souls,' he insisted. 'Unique opportunity. We hope to have long discussion about it tomorrow.'

Ignoring my continued protests, he turned and rejoined his companions, who had been waiting patiently for him a few feet away. Several of the torches had been extinguished by now, either by the wind or simply from lack of fuel; as the procession moved along the shore to the steps carved out of the cliffside that led up to the village, the remaining lights gradually failed as well, some in sudden clusters of three or four, others singly. The sight reminded me of a gigantic centipede, with glowing carbuncles dotted along its back: segment by segment it drifted into blackness

I resigned myself to my fate and settled down to rest on the sand, huddled into a corner where two nets came together and offered at least the illusion of security.

'And what did the souls have to say to you?'

I forced my eyes open and blinked hazily at the speaker.

A group of men had gathered at the outskirts of the nets and were gazing at me with calm detachment. It was shortly after dawn, a grey, dull morning, with a thick mist on the surface of the sea. I could see little more than ten yards in any direction, but a faint sucking sound, a gurgling as the small waves surged over the ridged bars of sand, lingered briefly, and retreated, made me horribly aware that the tide was advancing once more and was barely a dozen feet away from me

I scrambled painfully to my feet, my legs stiff and numb after the night's exposure and hardly able to support me. I clutched a strand of netting for support and stifled a groan of pain as the blood began to creep back to its accustomed channels.

'Get me out of here!'

The man who had spoken raised his hand. 'All in good time. First, we must know about our souls.'

I stared at him in bewilderment. The tide was edging closer to my feet and I looked desperately around for an exit. All the paths leading away from the centre, however, seemed to originate at the seaward side, no doubt circling round eventually to bring the wandering soul safely out on land, and, if I were to choose any of them, I would have to begin by wading through water that was ankle-deep already.

'Pull the nets down!' I gestured wildly with both hands, thrusting the palms downwards.

Ellicott shook his head. 'They must remain till one hour after dawn,' he remarked blandly. 'Till the first ray of sunlight strikes the cords. Do not worry. The depth of the tide is no greater than one metre.'

I had begun to shiver uncontrollably. My soaked shirt clung to my skin, my teeth chattered, my body surged with pain each time I attempted to move. 'What do you want to know?' I pleaded. The words emerged in single utterances, brief explosions forced out like coughs or groans.

'What our souls look like. What they said to you. What their plans are. Whether they are content with our arrangement.'

I had seen nothing, of course, during the night and, considering my predicament, had slept remarkably soundly. I could not even remember having dreamed. Nevertheless, I had to tell them something.

'Your souls,' I suggested desperately, 'are like bats. Each has a recognisable face, the face of its owner. They have wings. They swoop and flutter like bats. But they are beautiful, not sinister.'

I paused. The men nodded encouragingly. This seemed to be what they wanted to hear. 'Your souls are very intelligent,' I went on. 'We talked of many things. Of shoes and ships – ' I caught myself up in time and continued without any obvious change of direction: 'Philosophy, we talked of philosophy. Religion. The nature of God. How to lead a good life. Your souls are very wise.'

Once again the heads nodded in unison. I realised that I was close to delirium, thoughts were spinning incoherently around my head, totally irrelevant associations were thrusting themselves forward and demanding attention, and my body swayed like a half-demolished statue on the point of collapse. I struggled to finish before I lapsed into total absurdity and risked being abandoned once more: 'They are happy,' I told them, 'your souls are happy. They foresee good times for you, prosperity, contentment, healthy children, abundance of food and drink. You deserve all these because you care for your souls, you respect their wishes, you give them space to play and frolic. All souls should frolic,' I concluded lamely, aware of the inanity of the remark, but desperate to put an end somehow to my ordeal.

Ellicott stepped forward and made his way rapidly through the maze to my side. 'So he knew the route all along!' I remember thinking as I slumped helplessly into his arms. The water was already lapping around my feet. He began to drag me through the passage-way and several of his companions came to help him. I recall little else of that morning: the men hoisted me on their shoulders, forming a kind of bier, and began to carry me back to the village. The rising sun broke through a gap in the dark clouds and shot a ray of fierce heat straight into my eyes, causing me to gasp with pain. On entering the village, we passed a young woman carrying a shopping bag. She was dressed differently from the villagers and she stared at me curiously. The men carried me to the inn and put me to bed.

I have no idea how long I slept. The landlord told me three days; his wife said five. Both estimates seem improbable but, as my watch had somehow gone missing during the night of my ordeal, I have no way of checking. Either it was removed from my wrist by one of my bearers, or the strap loosened or broke and it fell off. There are no newspapers published in the village, of course, and none ever reach it from the outside world (or, if they do, they are so outdated that wars have been fought and won, revolutions have triumphed and been suppressed, governments have been overturned and monarchs fallen, long before any intimation of the mere possibility of the events has come to the villagers. Some of the older inhabitants, in the tavern, even talk as though Stalin and Churchill still flourished, and no one contradicts them, though I suspect that they refer now to mythic rather than historical figures). And, though my room possesses both a radio and a colour television, nothing happens when I turn the dials except a faint hiss, a crackling, a whisper as from other worlds striving to make themselves known but already aware of the futility and uselessness of the attempt.

The landlady brought me a meal. She is young, much younger than her husband, and astonishingly beautiful, despite the iron-grey hair which, when seen from behind, prepares one for an elderly, wrinkled, toothless grimace rather than the smooth, flawless features and the flash of perfect teeth. Perfect, however, only at first glance for, like the other villagers, she has filed them to sharp points that rouse vague feelings of unease, disquiet. Today, to my surprise, instead of the black cloak and hood that I have invariably seen her wearing, she was dressed in a simple white blouse and a dark-blue, pleated skirt. As she bent forward to adjust my bed-clothes, the loosely-fitting blouse dropped slackly away from her body to reveal a pair of perfect breasts, ripe and full, plump and swelling like carefully nurtured fruit at its peak. I could not prevent myself from gazing at them; she noticed this and, instead of retreating indignantly, merely held her pose a little longer and smiled at me encouragingly.

Tentatively, I stretched out my hand and cupped one of the breasts within it, the flimsy cotton intervening. Her smile broadened and she moved closer to the bed. I slipped my hand inside the blouse, gently caressed the warm skin, the hard, stiff nipple. She came nearer still, lay down on top of the bed and snuggled close to me.

The door opened and the landlord came in.

I struggled to a sitting position and attempted to push the woman away. To my amazement, she clung even

21

closer to me, smothering my face in kisses, muttering endearments, and nibbling my left ear-lobe. Finally I managed to extricate myself and prepared to encounter the wrath of an enraged and jealous husband. The landlord's face was indeed twisted into an extraordinary grimace that combined elements of anger, fear, and outrage, but his gaze was directed, not at myself or his dishevelled and panting wife, but at the mirror attached to the ramshackle dressing-table that, together with the bed, a chair, and a tiny bedside table, provided the only furnishings in the room.

When I first rented the room, I found the mirror covered by a thick black cloth that completely obscured it; naturally I removed this, in order to enable myself to carry out the normal requirements of my toilette, brushing my hair, adjusting my tie, and so on (even cleaning my teeth and shaving had to be performed in front of this mirror, for the tiny bathroom, crammed as an afterthought into a corner of the room, was totally deprived of one of its own). Whenever I returned to the room, I found that the cloth had been returned to its original position; I put up with this for a time and then, the evening before my ill-fated excursion to the beach, I had suddenly tired of playing my role in this meaningless farce and had bundled up the cloth and thrust it out of sight into one of the drawers.

The landlord had raised his left arm to shield his eyes and, turning his head to avoid a direct glance at the mirror, was jabbing in its direction with the forefinger of his right hand. 'My soul!' he bleated, 'he tries to steal my soul! Put back the cloth before he steals my soul!' Despite the air of extreme terror with which he spoke, I noticed that he persisted with his fractured English rather than, as would have been more normal, uttering his complaint in his own tongue. 'Where is the cloth?' he moaned. 'Give me the cloth!'

It was less pity, than disgust at this performance, and a desire to remove him from the room as quickly as possible, that prompted me to offer him assistance. I indicated to his wife where she could find the cloth and she stood up and strolled in a leisurely fashion across the room. I noticed that she seemed to have no fear of the mirror; in fact, she paused for a moment in front of it to adjust her hair and raise her blouse to cover her half-exposed breasts before stooping to open the drawer and take out the cloth.

Instead of replacing it herself, however, she tossed it contemptuously towards her quivering husband, so that it landed over his head and draped him for an instant like a veiled statue. 'Take your cloth,' she muttered. 'Save your soul with it if you can.' The extraordinary contempt in her voice convinced me that she must belong to the opposing faction to her husband, those who are concerned that their dreams are being tampered with, rather than the believers in the material existence of the soul. Keeping the cloth over his head to shield his eyes, the landlord lunged in the direction of the dressing-table, misjudging his distance to such an extent that he brought his knee into sharp contact with one of the large brass drawer-handles. He let out a yelp of pain, but managed to fling the cloth over the mirror and obscure it to his satisfaction, nevertheless.

He limped back across the room, clutching his injured knee with his right hand, and settled himself cautiously into the chair. I prepared myself to receive a torrent of vituperation and recrimination, but instead he sat silent for a few moments, beaming at me with unexpected benignity. I took the opportunity to scrutinise him more closely than I had been able to till now. He is a fat, sloppy sort of man, with heavy, unintelligent features; he speaks and moves slowly and laboriously, and he is habitually dressed in a filthy white shirt which he leaves sprawling half-open, revealing a chest matted with coarse black hairs. There is a deep scar on his left cheek that must have remained unattended too long, for it has only half-healed and one can see a pink ridge of flesh beneath the puckered skin.

He placed a hand on each knee and swayed confidentially towards me. 'So, Mr Everrich,' he wheezed, 'you want to sleep with my wife?' I began to utter an indignant denial, but he continued imperturbably, 'Well, go ahead. Enjoy yourself. I watch.' He settled back in the chair and gazed at me expectantly. I stared at him and then at the woman, who moved quickly back towards the bed, a smile of welcome on her face. She sat down beside me.

'No,' I said quickly, 'no, I don't want to sleep with her. That is – ' I paused, uncertain how to continue. Presumably I was faced with some local custom of offering wives to guests or visitors; I did not want to offend the woman, or even her husband (whose goodwill might be useful to me in my investigations) and yet I had no desire to perform the act in full view of a spectator. Perhaps he might be persuaded to leave (for, to be honest, I found the woman, who had begun to caress my hair and to snuggle close to me once more, extremely alluring), but the offer might be contingent upon the presence of an audience and might be withdrawn, in an atmosphere of insult and hostility, if I suggested an alteration of the normal ritual.

'I am very tired,' I apologised. 'I have not yet recovered from my ordeal. Perhaps some other time. When I am better.' To my relief, this seemed to satisfy him, for he waved his wife away from me and told her to leave the room. She obeyed with some reluctance, I thought, casting a lingering glance back at me as she passed through the doorway.

'Now,' said the landlord, as if the whole incident had never occurred, 'now I teach you Seahorse.' He pulled a pack of greasy playing cards from his pocket, shuffled them expertly, and began to deal them out on the foot of the bed.

I had watched the villagers playing this game in the evenings, in the local tavern, and had found it totally impossible to understand the rules, or even the basic principles on which it was based. Each player was allotted a certain amount of cards, which he then proceeded to hurl down upon the table, with great vehemence and in no discernible order or pattern, the whole being accompanied by an amazing collection of shrieks, grunts, yells, moans and shouts. The game also appears to involve the distribution of a collection of counters, all shades of blue and green, that are tossed into a central pile at strategic moments, though, once again, it is impossible for an outsider to understand just when and why this discarding becomes appropriate. The winner seems to be the player who disposes of his counters most quickly, even if he still holds several of his cards in his hand.

Meanwhile the landlord had finished dealing the cards and had hauled from his pocket a collection of the counters, tied up in a filthy, stained plastic bag by an intricate series of knots that he proceeded laboriously to unravel. Finally he had the bag open; he poured the counters on to the bedspread and began to distribute them. As he allocated each one he would mutter the word of a colour, 'olive', 'lime', 'aquamarine', 'sky-blue', 'leaf-green', 'magenta', and so on, and seemed to attach great importance to distributing a fixed amount of counters of each colour to each of us. Unfortunately, apart from the obvious extremes of 'sky-blue' and 'leaf-green', I found it impossible to make any distinction at all between the various colours: if they *did* differ, it was by such imperceptible degrees, each shade subtly merging and blending with its companion, that, strain as I might, I could make out nothing except an undifferentiated mass of greenish-blue.

The landlord hastily mumbled a few instructions, that I failed totally to comprehend, and proceeded to hurl down his first card, accompanying the motion with a blood-curdling yell of the kind delivered by a karate expert intent on unnerving his opponent. The card depicted a mermaid perched on a rock, combing her golden hair and gazing archly towards the photographer – I say 'photographer', for it had exactly the texture and look of a photograph, though I concluded immediately that it must be either an ingeniously presented painting or a posed and obvious fake.

I hesitated, staring at him blankly and wondering what move to make. He had already detached another card from his hand and held it poised for delivery, clearly expecting me to respond to his move with similar swiftness. Taking advantage of my delay, he tossed the card on top of his first one and, with a surprisingly nimble flutter of his thick fingers, seized a few discs from each of the half-dozen or so piles into which he had arranged his counters, and flung these too into the centre of the table. The new card showed a couple of lobsters, each still in the pot in which it had been trapped, glaring at each other with evident malice.

Again I gaped at him, unable to understand what was going on. I lowered my eyes to examine the cards I held in my hand and, when I raised them again, the landlord had disposed of half his cards and almost all his counters, flicking the latter on to the central pile in a dazzling flow of colour that caught the light and appeared to hang there like two lonely arches of a rainbow. As I watched, he completed the process, ridding himself of his remaining counters and settling back in his chair with a beam of satisfaction on his face and his hands folded complacently across his belly.

'You pretty stupid,' he informed me smugly. 'With us any fool can play Seahorse, even the insane.' I began to protest angrily that anyone who knows the rules of a game, who has played it all his life, who understands the codes and underlying structures, is naturally at an advantage over someone attempting it for the first time, and that the issue was merely one of familiarity and had nothing at all to do with intelligence.

'Take the transport system in any large city,' I argued. 'Each works in a different fashion: with some you buy a token, with others a ticket, in yet others you must have a pass. Some have a fixed fare, no matter the distance, others charge according to the area travelled. In this one you can throw away your ticket once you have passed the first barrier, it is no longer needed; in that one you must present it again as you leave and woe betide you if you *have* discarded it! In some cities you buy your ticket in a booth beforehand and punch holes in it by means of an ingenious machine in each compartment; in others you purchase a ticket on entrance and sometimes you will be given change and sometimes not. Now, obviously the native of each particular city, no matter how mentally impoverished he may be, possesses a superiority, *in this one respect only*, over the greatest genius from outside, who may find himself attempting to offer cash when he should have a token, or who has neglected to insert his ticket in the correct machine at the correct time. The official smiles at him pityingly from the security of his glass barrier, or mutters a few words of indignant contempt; behind him, the crowd, resenting the delay imposed on them by his ignorance, utters complaints, insults, even threats.

'No,' I continued, warming to my theme, 'you may imagine you have triumphed over me here but, put us in a different context, change the rules, instruct me properly in their application, and we will see who comes off best after all.' I paused, panting for breath, and not a little disconcerted to realise that the landlord, who sat nodding his head and smiling at me with the most extreme goodnature, had probably not taken in a word that I had spoken.

At this moment there was a knock at the door and, without waiting for an invitation, Hanslett barged into the room. He paused on seeing the landlord and then addressed himself to me, ignoring him completely. 'You conspire with them!' he accused me excitedly. 'You plan with them to trick us and deceive us!'

I gazed at him blankly.

'You were in our dreams!' he went on breathlessly. 'You sought to seduce our virgins in their dreams!'

I began to struggle out of bed, half-expecting, from his dishevelled appearance and the wild gleam in his eyes, that he was preparing to attack me. My movements disturbed the cards and the counters that the landlord had left lying on the bed, and several of the counters spilled on to the floor and rolled towards Hanslett's feet. The sight must have distracted him, for he suddenly lost all his belligerence and stooped to gather up the counters. He weighed them thoughtfully in his right hand and stared from them to the landlord, to me, and back at the counters.

'I teach him Seahorse,' the landlord explained.

'Seahorse!' It is impossible to express in writing the tone of utter contempt with which Hanslett repeated the word: '*Seahorse?*'

The landlord nodded. The bluster and self-confidence had drained out of him, and, with it, the materiality of his body had somehow shrunk too: he had become wizened and dwarfish and when, avoiding Hanslett's intent stare and yet keeping his face and body turned towards him, he rose from the bed and sidled apologetically out of the room, he appeared to have lost height and to be a good six inches shorter than when he had entered.

'The old fool!' Hanslett muttered, as the landlord closed the door behind him. 'So he thinks he has taught you Seahorse.'

I began to explain that the attempt had not been particularly successful in any case, but Hanslett ignored me. 'He calls this Seahorse,' he mused, flicking through the cards that remained on the bed and examining the order in which they had been deposited. Picking up the counters, he uttered a snort of disgust on discovering the division into eight separate shades that the landlord had effected. He turned towards me, clutching a fistful of counters and thrusting them almost into my face: 'Only imbeciles and cretins,' he told me, his voice shaking with sudden rage, 'play the game in this manner. It is an insult to a guest to tell him that is the true Seahorse. Debased, mindless. . . .' His voice trailed away into incoherent mutterings and then, when I thought he had finally fallen silent, he added unexpectedly: 'The village is full enough of them as it is. Centuries of inbreeding.'

He made an effort to control himself and sat down beside me on the bed. 'Look,' he explained, selecting eight counters and spreading them in front of me. 'Any fool, a child even, can see that these are different. No skill is needed to distinguish between them. Fifteen shades is the minimum, the absolute minimum, that can be used and yet retain self-respect. Real experts use fifty. Myself, I play with thirty-three.' He made the last statement in a tone of modest pride, as though I were expected to recognise the quality of his achievement. I wondered if I should seize him by the hand and congratulate him, but he went on, after a short pause, to tell me about the cards. 'This too is all wrong,' he argued, spreading out half a dozen of the cards in the order in which the landlord had arranged them: '*Tower*, for example, should never follow *Grotto*.' One card showed what was obviously the island opposite the village, seen from a distance of a few hundred yards, with a ruined tower prominent in the left-hand corner. The other presented what seemed to be a large cavern, filled with stalactites and stalagmites that had, over the centuries, congealed into a host of weird and grotesque formations. Both pictures were unmistakably photographs.

'And *Walkers on Water* and *Wolf Hunt* should never come into conjunction.' He showed me a picture of a group of children apparently walking on the surface of the sea, the waves lapping round their ankles. Next to this was a photo-card of the statue on the fountain in the village square, familiar enough to me by now, except that, instead of being worn and broken into a shapeless and unintelligible mass, it looked newly chiselled and displayed the final moments of a wolf hunt, the cornered animal's jaws open in a defiant snarl, dogs yapping at its feet, a spear piercing its face from cheek to cheek, the triumphant huntsman crouched low in the saddle, almost indeed hurling himself from his horse with the vigour of his thrust.

I studied the two cards carefully. Both were undoubtedly photographs and yet both represented physical impossibilities. The weathering of the statue, the crumbling away of its meaning and identity, must have been the process of several centuries: it was new hundreds of years ago, long before photography was invented. As for the children walking on the water, that could well be an ingenious fake, the subtle superimposition of two separate images to give the desired effect, though I had to confess that it had been expertly done and contained none of the usual clues that reveal a deception of this kind.

Satisfied with this explanation, I studied the second card once more. Knowing that it could not represent an actual scene, I found it easier to deduce that it too was probably the product of some kind of trickery: a model, perhaps of the original statue, that had been photographed against the actual background of the square, which was certainly itself authentic and modern enough, with some of the houses even sprouting the useless television aerials that had so intrigued me on my first entrance to the village.

Hanslett had been watching patiently as I examined the cards. I could, I suppose, have asked him to reveal the secret of their production, but I was wary of antagonising him by even hinting that they might not be authentic. No doubt the villagers took considerable pride in the skill and ingenuity that had created them, and they might well resent an outsider's questioning of their validity.

'You see now,' he said, as I handed them back, 'that everything that idiot taught you is worthless?' I replied that he had in fact taught me nothing, for I had been unable to understand his explanation of the rules.

Hanslett stared at me in amazement. 'But even a

child – ' he began. He broke off and rose to his feet, shaking his head in what was either sympathy or astonishment. 'I will visit you again tomorrow,' he said. He swept the cards and counters into a heap on the floor and moved towards the door. When he reached it, he turned and gazed at me steadily for a few seconds. 'Keep out of our dreams tonight,' he warned me. He closed the door softly behind him.

The next day I felt well enough to get up and go downstairs for a meal. As I had expected, the dining-room was empty: I am certainly the only guest in the hotel at the moment, and probably the only one in many months, if not years. The landlord's main source of income appears to be the tavern, further down the street, which he also owns, and where he is to be found each evening, presiding over the endless games of Seahorse, leaning back in his chair, hands planted firmly on his knees, and a smirk of insufferable complacency on his face.

His wife brought me my meal, fresh red mullet, grilled to perfection, with a slice of lemon and new potatoes. Once again she was wearing that distractingly provocative blouse and, as she stooped to place my dish before me, she shot me an unmistakable glance of invitation. She straightened up and made her way back to the kitchen, pausing at the door to direct an arch smile at me, and a sly lift of the eyebrows.

I hesitated, wondering whether to follow her. The meal looked and smelled almost unbearably delicious, and would be the first solid food I had tasted in several days. I hated the idea of letting it go to waste and began to eat hastily, scarcely even chewing in my anxiety, and keeping an eye fixed on the outer door, through which the landlord could be expected to return. From the kitchen came the sound of running water and the clatter of dishes being piled together.

I finished quickly, pushed back my chair as quietly as possible, and walked cautiously to the kitchen door. She stood with her back towards me, bent over the sink. As she stretched out her hands to pick up a pile of dishes to her right, I stole up behind her and clasped my hands round her, caressing her breasts.

She gasped in surprise and dropped the dishes into the sink, where almost all of them shattered at once. A cup bounced off the rim and landed, miraculously unhurt, on the floor, where it spun happily for several seconds before subsiding in a series of rattles and then, quite unexpectedly, splitting into two perfect halves. She whirled round and pushed me violently away, sending me sprawling against the far wall and knocking the breath completely from my body. Her teeth flashed in an alarming and dangerous grimace, but she said nothing. She placed her hands on her hips and glared at me.

Her silence unnerved me. I wondered whether this resistance was part of the foreplay to which the villagers were accustomed and whether I was expected to return to the attack and grapple with her once more. And if so, how long was the pattern of advance and rejection expected to continue; to what extent was the use of force sanctioned or even approved of; was blood perhaps destined to flow before the final union took place? Or had I simply misread the signals, interpreting as an invitation what was merely a smile of welcome, the standard and meaningless response of hostess to customer? (though, after the events of the previous day, that seemed highly unlikely). Or had I, as so often in the past, merely missed my opportunity, delaying too long, neglecting to act on the instant, offering an unintended and negligent insult and so causing the invitation to be abruptly withdrawn?

I had been misled perhaps by the blouse, taking that to indicate availability, making the familiar mistake of confusing the literal and the metaphorical, mentally associating 'loose blouse' and 'loose woman'. And the blouse itself might have one connotation when worn in a bedroom and another (comfort, coolness, ease of movement) when worn in a kitchen.

Meanwhile the landlady had turned her back on me, in an unmistakably dismissive gesture, and had begun to gather up the broken pieces of crockery. I thought of offering to help her, but decided that this might lead to more complications than I felt qualified to handle at the moment. I turned to leave the kitchen and, as I did so, the woman spoke, though without moving to face me: 'Your salad is on the table.'

She was quite right; it stood within reach of my right hand. I picked it up and returned to the dining-room.

When I had finished my meal, I decided to take a stroll through the village and down to the beach. It was early afternoon, the sun high in a cloudless sky, but with a cool breeze that occasionally made me shiver and almost prompted me to return to the hotel for an extra sweater. I wished to avoid any further encounters for the moment with either the landlady or her husband, however, and I decided to continue in the hope that the wind would soon die down.

I passed the statue in the village square and, remembering its role in the game of Seahorse, I stopped to examine it more closely. Without the clue that the card had given me, I would have found it impossible to interpret it as a hunting scene, and, even with that association in mind, it was difficult enough to fit the remaining fragments into the requisite pattern. There were segments of what might be a spear or a staff, certainly; a standing or seated figure; and a shapeless mass at the bottom of the composition that might indeed be a wolf – and might well be almost anything else, into the bargain.

I shrugged my shoulders and gave up the attempt to interpret it. The breeze had died away and the sun was becoming uncomfortably hot. I thought I would approach the beach by a different route from the usual one, following the path along the cliff-top in the opposite direction to the Institute for a time, then working my way down to shore level. I soon left the village behind me, and was struck by the utter silence that lay upon the landscape, and the lack of any sign of human life in the fields or in the farmhouses that were dotted across the narrow strip of land between the coast and the mountains. Once, to be sure, I passed one of these houses and was startled by a huge black dog that had lain in wait inside its kennel, choosing to burst out suddenly just as I drew level and to hurl itself ferociously towards my throat. Fortunately it was checked at the last moment by a chain that brought it to an abrupt halt less than a foot away from me, so that hot drops of spittle sprayed my face and shoulder. The animal fell back on its hindquarters, snarling, then launched itself towards me once more, only to be thwarted again by the chain. The shock of the impact should have been enough to choke it, but it paid no attention to this, resuming the attack as long as I remained within sight and hearing, its barks changing to growls, and finally dwindling to frustrated squeals and whimpers as it saw its opportunity vanishing.

I retreated, trembling, wiping the drops of slaver from my skin and grateful that the chain had held firm, though wondering at the mentality of people who could keep such an obviously vicious and dangerous beast within easy reach of innocent passers-by: another two paces to the right and the beast's jaws would have been on my throat – and even at that distance I would still have been within the nominal limits of the pathway. I looked back once or twice to see if the commotion had brought the inhabitants out of doors, determined to return and give them a piece of my mind if they did appear, but the house remained totally silent and as if deserted.

A few hundred yards after this, I heard another sound, metal grinding against stone, the noise of something being struck or shattered. I turned a corner and came in sight of a group of men engaged in breaking rocks by the side of the path. They were stripped to the waist, their backs burnt almost black by the sun; as they bent over to swing their picks, the ridge of their spines stood out sharply under the skin. One or two of them glanced quickly at me, but they showed little interest in my presence and none of them spoke.

I was about to move on when I noticed that one of them was wearing a watch that looked exactly like the one I had lost. I hesitated a moment and then asked him if I could have a look at it. Without a word, he unstrapped it and handed it to me.

I turned it over and over, examining it. There was no doubt whatever that it was mine: it was the same make, it told the date and temperature as well as the time, it even had my initials scratched on the back. I gazed at the man, who had stopped work and was leaning on the handle of his pick, staring calmly at me. The others too had decided to take a rest and surveyed me curiously.

The men had so much the air of a group of convicts, completing a stint of hard labour, that I looked instinctively for a guard or warder, someone in authority to whom I could appeal for help in my predicament. No one offered to assist me, however, and all seemed to be working on an equal footing. I felt that I should proceed cautiously: I was isolated and outnumbered and had no means of defending myself if the men should turn hostile. On the other hand, I had no intention of tamely surrendering my property, though it did occur to me that the watch might have been taken – in the eyes of the villagers at least – quite legitimately, as a reward for the assistance that had been offered to me, a type of salvage that might be perfectly justified in local custom.

'That's a fine watch,' I offered, feeling out my ground. 'Did you buy it here, in the village?'

The man smiled. 'It was given to me,' he said, 'by my grandfather. A family heirloom.'

'Are these his initials on the back, then, or yours?' I enquired. I had not intended to pose the question so bluntly, but the man's self-confidence provoked me.

'Yes,' he agreed.

I paused and glanced again at his companions, most of whom were grinning openly and obviously enjoying my discomfiture. 'It's a fine watch,' I repeated, 'a very fine watch.' He held out his hand to receive it back. I offered it to him slowly, but retained my grip on the strap, so that it oscillated between us for a few seconds, as though forming the centre of a miniature tug-of-war. 'It must be good to have a watch like that,' I continued. 'If I were you, I should take good care of it, in case it gets stolen.'

He gave an almost imperceptible tug and I released my hold on the strap. 'I'll do that,' he agreed, as he fastened it on to his wrist, 'though I'm sure that you must be aware by now that theft is totally unknown in this village.'

He lifted up his pick and prepared to return to work. 'My grandfather,' he remarked pleasantly, as he hoisted it on to his shoulder, 'also gave me a pen that writes under water. It has a light too, so that you can use it in the dark. It's a very wonderful pen. Would you like to see that too?'

Involuntarily, I slapped my hand to my breast pocket, for I too have a pen exactly like that and it occurred to me that he must have appropriated it as well, at the same time as he took my watch. But the pen was still there, I could feel its familiar shape and the pressure of its slim metallic form against my chest. Noticing my gesture, the men burst into a roar of laughter; they turned their backs to me and resumed their task, whistling cheerfully. The man who had spoken to me lingered a little longer, as though challenging or expecting me to continue the conversation; when I said nothing, he shrugged and took his place beside his companions.

I continued along the path, reflecting on this incident and wondering if I should, or could, have acted differently, more decisively perhaps, and so have recovered my property. Absorbed in reverie, I hardly noticed that a man had scrambled out of the ditch a few yards ahead of me, and was rushing towards me waving his arms vigorously, until he was almost on top of me. I backed away from him, ready to turn and flee, and at the same time searching for some means of defence; but he came to an abrupt halt less than a yard away from me, drew himself up on the very tips of his toes, and leaned forward to touch me lightly with his forefinger, just over the heart.

I stared at him in amazement. Though he shared the general characteristics and overall appearance of almost all the males in the village, I was certain that I had never seen him before, and I had no idea what he wanted with me.

'I am Ellicott,' he said. 'You remember me. You come with me.'

He was perhaps a relative, or another person of the same name, for he most certainly could not be the Ellicott I had encountered a few days previously. He seized my arm and began to hustle me towards the edge of the cliff, where the path descended precipitously towards the shore. I attempted to resist; I dug my heels into the hard-baked mud and endeavoured to shake myself free of his grasp; but he carried me with him relentlessly. At last I begged him to pause for a moment, to allow me to pull myself together and re-arrange my dishevelled clothing. I hoped too that he might take the opportunity to explain his strange behaviour.

As we stood on the cliff-top, the man who had taken my watch, and a couple of his companions, strolled past us, laughing and chuckling over some private joke. When he caught sight of me, the man raised his left arm and waved it in a derisory and triumphant gesture, so that the sunlight slanted off the gold casing of the watch. He shouted something that I failed to catch.

'Is that watch yours?' demanded 'Ellicott'. I confessed that it was, that I had attempted to recover it and had been thwarted.

'Why didn't you just ask for it?' He looked amazed. 'You needed only to say: "I claim what is due to me: give it to me, right hand to right hand." You stretch out your right hand, he puts the watch into it. Nothing could be easier.'

'And how could I be expected to know that?' I responded angrily. 'If all thefts were as easily disposed of as that, life would be very simple!'

'But you know the formula surely?' he asked, staring at me strangely. 'We used to use it all the time at school.'

I was struck by the phrasing of that remark, though I had no time to reflect on it. And besides, his words did, in a very curious manner, conjure up an apparent memory: I seemed to recollect a code of that kind from my school-days, though the exact phrasing was rather different.

'Ellicott' went on to tell me that the man and his companions had been placed where I had found them, for a very definite purpose. The village custom was that, whenever anyone was known to have committed a theft, he was sent to work at that particular place for three consecutive days, and had to display prominently, on or near his person, the objects he had stolen. If the owner of the goods passed and claimed his property, it was returned to him on the spot, and the culprit was obliged to perform whatever penance, or whatever act of restitution, that the victim (within reason) demanded. If the owner did not come by, or if he appeared but did not recognise or claim what belonged to him, the thief was released and allowed to keep what he had stolen.

I said that, in that case, I would pursue the criminal and insist on recovering my property after all, but 'Ellicott' shook his head and told me that I had missed my chance. If the thief succeeded in brazening the matter out, or in intimidating the rightful owner, on the first occasion, the matter was considered at an end and no further action could be taken, even if the thief made public confession of his crime at a later date.

He took me by the arm once more and said that it was now time for us to go fishing. When I asked what he was talking about, he said that I had acknowledged myself his partner for the day and was now legally bound to accompany him to help collect his lobsters. No boat was allowed to leave the shore unless it had a crew of at least two, and his usual assistant, who had been drinking heavily the previous evening, had collapsed into the ditch just a few yards away from where we had met and was therefore unable to accompany him. The law provided that, in such a situation, a fisherman was empowered to seize the first able-bodied man he encountered and force him to go instead, no matter how urgent the business or personal affairs of the other might be. My only recourse would have been to flee the moment I saw him, for the second he touched me the conditions of the law came into effect, and my accompanying him thus far had merely strengthened the bond between us.

I objected bitterly, though to no effect, that it was wrong to take advantage of a man's ignorance and innocence in such a way, to force him to comply with customs and regulations that had never even been explained to him; but he merely shrugged and said that we would have to hurry if we were to be back before nightfall.

He led me down the path to the beach – I slithering on the loose stones, struggling to keep my balance, and clutching desperately at shrubs and tufts of grass whenever I felt it impossible to stay upright any longer; 'Ellicott' stepping confidently and sure-footedly, occasionally dragging impatiently on my arm when I was delaying him to a more than usual extent. We reached the beach and he led me towards his boat, which had been left high on the shingle.

I helped him haul it down into the water and he held it steady for me while I climbed in. He emptied at my feet the evil-smelling contents of the canvas bag he had carried with him all this time: I could distinguish rotting pieces of eel and mackerel, all probably several days old. Noticing my discomfort, as I tried to seat myself as far away from them as possible, he said with a smile that the older the bait was, the more it stank, and the better the lobsters liked it. He began to row us out into the bay: close to the shore the water was filthy with fragments of driftwood, rusty cans, decayed seaweed and a scum of discarded oil; then it cleared to a bright blue through which you could see the ridged sand of the bottom, and, about two hundred yards out, this gradually changed, through almost imperceptible gradations, to darker shades of blue, a mixture of blue and green, and finally a sombre and murky type of true green.

He rowed for some time in silence, steering towards open water, and once we were well out in the bay he started up the outboard motor. The wind blustered around us, and the clouds tossing in front of the sun made the water a constant patchwork of dark and light; as we left the protection of the headland the boat began to pitch and plunge in the waves in a manner I found most alarming. I regretted not bringing my sweater with me, for I was soon chilled through and huddled, shivering, in the bow of the boat.

'Ellicott' shouted something to me, but his words were carried off by the wind. I made gestures of incomprehension and he pointed vigorously at the locker beneath my feet. I opened it and pulled out a heavy pullover that had clearly lain there for weeks and had become thoroughly impregnated with the stench of rotten bait. He signalled to me to put it on and, with a particularly vicious gust of wind thrusting through me at that very moment, I felt I had little choice but to comply. The sweater was almost solid with dirt and grease, it hung stiffly around me, and the sharp collar jabbed painfully into my neck each time I attempted to move. The smell was indescribable and, after a few moments, I achieved a temporary relief from my miseries by vomiting quietly over the side.

At last we came to the first series of lobster pots, and he told me to hold the rudder while he hauled them up out of the water. The first two were empty and the unused bait lay congealed in a heavy mass on the bottom; he instructed me to clear this out and replace it with some we had brought with us. I obeyed, my throat thick with retching, but so dry now that nothing would come up. He observed me quietly, an enigmatic smile on his lips and, when I had finished, remarked that I had surely handled worse before: what about that centipede at school, for example?

I sat bolt upright and stared at him. I remembered the incident he must be referring to, for it was one of the most vivid from my schooldays, but I had no idea how he could have come to know anything about it. Before I could reply, he restarted the engine and moved on to the next pot. A huge lobster squatted in this, glaring at me malignantly, and I refused point blank when he ordered me to reach in and take it out. With a contemptuous grimace, he pulled it out himself and tossed it at my feet. I wriggled away in an instinctive attempt to place myself out of reach of its ferocious claws, almost overturning the boat in the process and forcing 'Ellicott' to grasp desperately at the rim to keep his balance.

We found six lobsters in that area, all of which 'Ellicott' removed himself, and continued on to the next. The creatures lay in a pile in the centre of the boat, the water still glistening on the dappled blue of their shells, waving their claws and antennae in a dispirited fashion. Occasionally one would drag itself free of the heap and crawl a few inches through the water that had gathered in the bottom of the boat before becoming tangled in a piece of netting or collapsing from exhaustion, eyes glittering balefully, until 'Ellicott' knocked it back into place with a sweep of his boot. I performed this service for him once or twice myself, though I was still wary of attempting to approach one with my hand.

The three lobsters we found there appeared to satisfy my companion, and we moved on to the final hunting ground. Here we made a discovery that utterly delighted him, causing him to break out into the first spontaneous smile of sheer joy that I had seen in any of the villagers: two monstrous lobsters were trapped in the same cage, each withdrawn into a corner and surveying the other warily. He muttered something about 'the duel of the lobsters' and stretched in his hand to remove one of them. It jabbed at him spitefully with its claw, almost making contact, so that he withdrew his hand hurriedly and sat for a moment nursing it thoughtfully. He made another attempt, but with unaccustomed caution, and the beasts seemed to take heart from this, both scuttling towards him in vicious triumph and forcing him to retreat ignominiously once more.

He decided finally to cut the pot loose and bring it home with us in the boat; he set it in the stern, close to his feet and as far away from the others as possible, as if he feared that the spirit of revolt and subversion might contaminate them too. And indeed something of this sort appeared to happen, for the half-dead creatures in the bottom of the boat began to squirm and wriggle as though endowed with a new vitality. They began to make bolder and bolder forays, and it was as much as I could achieve to keep them at bay by poking at them repeatedly with my foot.

Then I noticed that the two lobsters in the pot had abandoned their brief alliance and had begun to grapple fiercely with each other. I drew 'Ellicott's' attention to this and he shouted that I should try to separate them. I began to pick my way through the swirling mass of lobsters in the centre of the boat, but was forced to retreat when they stabbed at my legs and feet, which were protected only by a thin pair of trousers and a pair of canvas shoes.

The beasts in the pot were now locked in mortal combat. 'Ellicott' screamed at me once again to intervene and even risked upsetting the boat by darting forward once or twice from his seat in the stern to seize a lobster and flick it rapidly overboard before scrambling back to his position. The wind was rising again, however, gusting the boat into a dangerous and unpredictable equilibrium with the waves, and his attention was quickly reclaimed by his efforts to keep us on course. He signalled to me to continue with the task of hurling the other lobsters overboard so that I would have a clear path to the pot, which was now violently swaying and rocking as the combat increased in intensity.

The rescue of these two creatures appeared to mean so much to him that I nerved myself to the distasteful task and plunged my hand at random into the heap before me. My fingers closed round something hard and firm and, scarcely daring to look at it, I tugged it free and heaved it quickly over the side. 'Ellicott' yelled something in approval or encouragement and I continued blindly with my task, averting my head and even closing my eyes, knowing that if I once paused to consider what I was doing, I would find myself unable to continue. Pluck and heave, dart and flick: I counted six successful forays and, adding those to 'Ellicott's' earlier raids, I judged the immediate danger at an end and thought it safe to open my eyes. As I worked, I heard the water slap with increasing force against the side of the boat, which tossed and pitched in a quite terrifying manner; there was also a curious sound of grinding from the lobster pot, as the beasts hammered at each other, their claws skidding and grating fearfully as they sought a vulnerable spot.

I clutched the sides of the boat to steady myself, and stared around. Dirty water swirled and rocked in shallow pools through which one pitiful survivor scrabbled list-lessly and aimlessly for shelter. At that moment, the wind died abruptly away and this coincided exactly with a sudden silence from the lobster pot as the enraged creatures there finally succeeded in tearing each other to pieces. I stared at the scattered fragments of flesh, the shards of claw and shell; my gaze travelled onwards to meet that of 'Ellicott'. I expected him to shout, to curse, to condemn me for my tardy and ineffectual intervention, but, though his grey eyes surveyed me long and thought-fully, he said nothing. Finally he shrugged his shoulders and turned away from me to restart the engine. He began to steer us back towards the shore, his eyes fixed straight ahead, ignoring me.

As we swept round the headland and back into the shelter of the bay, I noticed that, despite the inclement weather, a young woman was sunbathing on the rock jut-ting furthest out into the water. Her legs from the thighs down were submerged in the sea and the part of her body that was visible was completely naked. Unlike the village women, she had fair, even golden hair, and I wondered if she might belong to the Institute. I drew my com-panion's attention to her and asked if he recognised her, but he seemed not to have heard me, or at any rate made no response.

When we arrived at the shore, he jumped out, making no attempt to secure his vessel or to gather up his gear, and strode briskly away across the beach. I hesitated a moment and then felt it my duty to draw the boat more securely on to the sand and fasten it to a post that stuck there at a weirdly slanting angle. When I was ready to follow him, he was almost out of sight, a tiny black dot skimming up the steps like a water beetle on the surface of the waves.

It was time, I felt, to make an assault on the Institute. I had been in the village now for days, perhaps even weeks, and had not so much as seen one of the occupants, unless I could count the woman I had glimpsed in my half-delirious state on the morning following my ordeal among the nets. I had arrived with no fixed plan, hoping that cautious enquiries among the villagers would give me some clues and suggest a suitable method of approach; the almost superstitious terror with which they regard the place, however, had offered me nothing except a collection of old wives' tales, beliefs that were obviously nonsensical and could bear no relation to the work that was actually performed there. I could not even discover how many scientists were present: some informants would tell me a precise number, four, six, eight, or whatever, always carefully detailing an exact proportion of men to women and always offering a different figure from their predecessors or successors; others would gaze at me blankly, then hold up all their fingers in rapid succession, 'Many,' they would mumble, 'many'.

I thought it might be best simply to take a stroll in the direction of the Institute, hoping to meet one of its inhabitants on the way. I could scarcely present myself as a casual visitor to the area, having already been in the village for so long a time; but I could perhaps offer an approximation to the truth by claiming an interest in the customs and behaviour of the local people. On the way out of the hotel, however, I was waylaid by the landlord, who seized me by the arm and began to drag me along the street to the tavern, insisting that, once again, he was going to teach me Seahorse.

I struggled to release myself, I even cursed him and threatened to strike him if he would not let go, but he paid no attention to me. A group of his cronies were already seated at one of the outdoor tables, engrossed in a game. The landlord pushed me into their midst and forced me to sit down in a chair. Someone thrust a few cards into my hand and spread some counters out before me; meanwhile the game had scarcely paused to receive me: cards were hurled on the table-top to the accompaniment of the usual howls and yells, counters were tossed on to the central pile with a rapidity that almost dazzled me.

I stared uncomprehendingly at the cards before me. One of them was familiar – Hanslett had called it *Walkers on Water* – and another, that of two lobsters trapped in a pot, was also recognisable, though this time both were in the same cage and previously, if I remembered correctly, they had been in separate ones. What most astonished me, though, was to discover that one card represented a a huge black dog, identical in every respect to the one that had attempted to attack me, lunging towards the camera (for this too appeared to be a photograph), its jaws open, teeth bared to strike, its mad eyes gleaming with hatred, and – I shuddered to realise – no chain to restrain it on this occasion.

The man to my right nudged me sharply in the ribs, almost causing me to drop my cards. 'Play!' he hissed. 'You have the advantage on us all.' When I still hesitated, he uttered a snort of contempt and plucked from my hand the card representing the dog while, with virtually the same movement, he swept up almost all my counters and flung them into the central heap. His action drew outraged protests from his fellow players; he defended himself vigorously, rising to his feet and thumping the table with a massive fist, so that it rocked and swayed alarmingly. The others crowded round him, clutching handfuls of counters in their fists and shaking them threateningly in his face; the landlord too was caught up in the argument and I took the chance to slip away unnoticed and made my way, almost at a run, to the outskirts of the village.

The noise and clamour behind me died away and soon I was walking in complete silence, apart from the endless murmur of the cicadas and the distant scream of seagulls from the beach. The fields on either side of me glowed with the wild flowers that, at this time of year, crowd out the crops in this area, turning the landscape into a mosaic of red, yellow, blue, white and purple, interspersed with the brown of the earth, the green of the grass. I began the ascent of the steep, narrow path that leads up to the Institute and, to my delight, I noticed that a figure was coming down the path from the building, towards me. As it came nearer, I realised that it was a woman and, nearer still, I recognised the person I had encountered a few mornings previously.

As we drew level, I greeted her. 'Fine morning,' I offered cordially.

She stopped and examined me curiously. 'You're the stranger,' she said. 'Why are you still here?'

I was disconcerted by her directness and, for a few moments, could think of no reply. Finally, 'Is there any law against visitors?' I enquired weakly.

She ignored my question. 'When are you leaving?' she asked.

I attempted a laugh. 'Not for some time yet,' I protested. 'I have work to do here.'

'Oh. You are studying the villagers then?'

'Yes.'

'They are not worth studying. The few who are not cretins are morons. They have lived in isolation too long. Go away and leave them to die out in peace.'

'But why are you here then?'

'We have a job to do.' As if even this neutral comment had revealed too much, she took me by the arm and turned me, gently and almost imperceptibly, to face in the same direction as herself. She set off down the road again, guiding me with her. I turned to look back at the Institute, more inaccessible than ever now, and would have hesitated, but she bore me irresistibly along with her.

'You work for Dr – what *is* his name again?' I probed.

'Denials.' That was how the word came out at first and then she immediately corrected herself: 'Daniels.'

'You assist him with his experiments?'

She made no reply.

I was both unwilling to give up so easily and provoked by the casual ease with which she had thwarted me. I decided to challenge her openly. 'It is curious,' I suggested, 'how badly I have slept since I came here. Each night my sleep is tormented by dreams, by nightmares. Strange shapes rise up to threaten me, I am menaced by unknown and previously unimagined terrors, misshapen creatures gibber at me and mock me. I awake shaken, drained of all energy and will-power, the cold dawn filters through my window, I shiver. Have you any idea what might cause this?'

'None whatever,' she remarked, 'unless there is something in the air or the climate that disagrees with you. Perhaps, if you returned to your homeland, these nightmares would disappear.'

'On the other hand,' I continued, ignoring this in my turn, 'it often seems to me that, for want of a better word to express it, my *soul* goes wandering at night here. It detaches itself from my body and flutters like some nocturnal creature, perhaps a bat, across the sand, skims the moon-flecked tips of the waves, rising and falling in perfect symmetry with the water beneath. Its destination, I believe, is the island which, as we turn this bend in the path, has just come into view, though what it should wish to perform there I can scarcely imagine.'

'Neither can I,' she agreed. 'Possibly you are suffering from indigestion, for it is a well-known fact that a diet made up almost exclusively of sea food can have unfortunate effects on those unaccustomed to large quantities of molluscs, crustacea, and aquatic creatures generally. Another reason, doubtless, for you to leave this area, where your health is evidently threatened, and to return to a more congenial and suitable environment.'

'Doubtless. The wind arising from the sea is ruffling my hair to an extent that I find intolerable. I hate to appear dishevelled, especially when I find myself in company as charming as that which I am enjoying at present. May I enquire, therefore, whether you possess a mirror so that, after I have run a comb casually through my hair, I could check whether I have restored myself to my normal, at least minimally tidy condition?'

She rummaged briefly in her handbag. 'I could have sworn,' she mused, 'that I placed a mirror here this morning, in fact I can clearly visualise myself doing so. For some inexplicable reason, however, it appears to have vanished.'

We had by now entered the village and were passing the church, with its elaborately decorated façade, the portal festooned with stone flowers, animals, and faces, the spire tiered and webbed like a gigantic wedding-cake. And, on either side, the dilapidated houses of the inhabitants, the plaster peeling and crumbling from the walls to reveal the mismatched layers of paint with which previous generations had attempted to delay the ravages of time, the ill-fitting shutters rocking gently in the almost imperceptible breeze.

We walked by the tavern, where the argument had apparently been settled and the players had returned to their game. The man who had provoked the hostility by playing my card for me glanced up as we passed, but gave no sign of recognition. I asked my companion where she was going, for, though I assumed she had come out to buy provisions, she seemed to have no particular destination in mind and did not even carry a shopping bag with her.

'To the butcher's first, I suppose,' she answered vaguely, almost as if at random. 'It's over here, isn't it?' We turned into a narrow, tiny street, perpetually darkened by the fact that the houses all jutted out abruptly at the second-storey level to form what was virtually an archway. The butcher's was locked and there was no sign of life but, as if she were accustomed to this, the woman led me round the back and knocked at a window. A man opened the back door and, when she explained what she wanted, he invited us in.

We passed through a cluttered living-room, filthy with disorder and neglect. Some wilted plants stood on the window-sill, as if deliberately placed there to ensure that whatever feeble remnants of light had filtered through from the street should be kept firmly at bay. I squashed something nameless underfoot, probably the remains of a meal, and, as I jerked involuntarily away from this and momentarily lost my balance, I thrust my hand down on the back of a chair to steady myself. My fingers grazed the thinning hair of an old man who sprawled there, his jaw hanging slackly open, his hands draped loosely over its meagrely padded arms. He made no movement as I touched him and, in the dim light, I could not even tell whether he was alive or dead.

The butcher led us into the shop, which communicated directly with the house. The shutters were closed, the air fetid with the noonday heat. As the villagers seemed to exist entirely on fish, I had not even been aware that meat was sold locally, and I looked around me with some anticipation. There seemed to be nothing for sale, however, except a couple of pathetically thin carcasses dangling from hooks, lambs, I assumed, or possibly goats. A grey heap of what looked like innards was stacked on a chopping-board on the counter and, apart from that, I could see nothing except a dozen bird cages suspended from the ceiling, each with its forlorn, chirping inhabitant.

'I didn't think they went in much for pets here,' I remarked to my companion, remembering the mangy dogs I had observed skulking at the corners of alleyways and trying to recollect whether I had even seen a cat during my stay.

'They eat them,' she replied contemptuously. 'They're considered a delicacy here.'

I stared again at the cages. To my untrained eye, they contained nothing but common songbirds, thrushes and robins and the like, none of them capable of offering more than a morsel for a human appetite. I wondered whether I should offer to buy them and set them free, but decided that, in their present weakened and apathetic state, they would fall easy victim to the first predator that came along. 'They snare them?' I enquired. 'In nets?'

She nodded.

'Like souls,' I almost added, but restrained myself in time.

Meanwhile, she had been negotiating with the butcher in a low voice, speaking so rapidly that I could make out nothing of what she said. I half-expected him to produce something from beneath the counter, with a triumphant flourish, a leg of pork perhaps, a turkey, or a boar's head, but, to my surprise, the woman turned abruptly and walked to the door without buying anything. The shop-keeper scurried anxiously round the counter and unlocked the door to the street. She stepped out without glancing at him and without a word of farewell, and I followed close behind her.

Dim as it was, the light in the street almost dazzled by comparison with the darkness inside; as we turned back to the centre of the village we seemed to walk into an oblong blaze of sunlight at the end of the alleyway that blinded me, and forced me to close and blink my eyes. I stumbled on a cobblestone and reached my hand to-wards her to support myself; she shook me impatiently away.

This gesture, coming on top of the mystery with which she had surrounded herself since we met, seemed gratui-tously offensive and I decided the time had come for a confrontation. 'You people must be really popular here,' I sneered, 'if you patronise all the local tradesmen as generously as this. Whom do we favour with our pres-ence next? And by the way,' I continued, without giving her a chance to reply, 'shouldn't we at least tell each other our names?'

'*Miss* Mason,' she replied gravely and with what seemed a ludicrously formal emphasis on the title. When I told her my name, she repeated it with what could only have been intentional misunderstanding. 'Overage?' she mused. 'Well, in some respects, you look it.'

I was too angry even to attempt a response and, as we

were just outside the hotel, I said brusquely that I had to leave her. 'Wait a minute,' she replied quickly, holding out her hand to restrain me and even, I thought, caressing me slightly, 'let me come in with you. It's important that I see your room.'

I stared at her in amazement. Her features had suddenly altered: from displaying aloof and almost hostile impassivity, they had become tender, compliant, even pleading. 'Let me come up,' she whispered, and this time she did stroke my arm, moving her fingers gently from shoulder to elbow. 'Just for a minute.' The change made her almost attractive: the round, freckled face, with its close-cropped brown hair was warm and vibrant, the half-opened lips looked moist and warm.

'All right,' I agreed. The landlady was in the foyer, sitting behind the desk as if the impossible might one day happen and she should be required to register another guest. I mumbled something about 'a friend' as we passed, and she examined us briefly and impassively before lowering her eyes to attend to her knitting. I led the way upstairs and unlocked my room.

As soon as she entered, she uttered something between a gasp and a snort and rushed to fling the window open. 'How can you *live* like this?' she panted, turning her back to it and leaning against the sill as she breathed deeply. 'You must suffocate in here.'

She seemed, like the landlord earlier, with his exaggerated concern for the mirror, to be overplaying her distress; and I remembered that she had shown no discomfort in the almost intolerably stale and nauseating atmosphere of the butcher's home and shop. 'It's the best room in the hotel,' I told her, 'or so the landlord assured me.'

'I can't stand this,' she muttered. 'I can't move without

my clothes sticking to me.' Her gaze roamed round the room and fastened on the tiny alcove that served as a bathroom. 'Is there a shower in there?' she wondered.

'Yes, but you can't – ' Before I could finish she had plunged towards it, pushing me aside as I attempted half-heartedly to block her way. She flung aside the bead curtain at the entrance and peered inside. 'This will do,' she said. 'I won't be a moment.'

'You can't do that,' I protested. 'It leaks, there is no rim to hold the water inside, you'll only flood the place.' This indeed was true, as I had discovered on my only attempt to use the shower since my arrival. 'And there's no hot water,' I added, my voice trailing into incoherence as she began to strip off her dress and tossed it, crumpled and turned inside-out, towards me. I caught it and began automatically to straighten it, for the habits of tidiness hammered into me at boarding-school have remained with me ever since. She wore nothing underneath the dress except a pair of flimsy underpants, which she also removed and threw, without even turning her head, in my direction. I caught these too and placed them neatly on top of the dress, which I had folded over my arm.

She had a short, stocky figure, sturdy rather than plump, and I caught a glimpse of firm, well-rounded breasts as she stepped into the alcove. She turned on the water and I heard a gasp and a stifled scream as it made its first impact. 'I told you it was cold,' I commented with morose satisfaction, but she made no reply. There were more gasps, moans, cries, shrieks, splutterings, bubblings, and then the sound of slaps as she directed the flow of water around her body; finally came sighs of contentment, even pleasure. Unexpectedly, she began to sing.

I noticed that a trickle of water had begun to work its way out of the alcove and was spreading across the floor.

I called to inform her of this, but she appeared not to hear me and I hesitated to poke my head through the bead curtain and tell her directly. The water widened into a fair-sized stream and then a puddle; it seeped remorselessly towards the door, moving in a series of small eddies that advanced, paused, and surged forward again, gaining strength after each interval. I felt powerless to intervene and could only hope that she would finish her shower before the water could reach the hallway, or even, and the thought struck me in a vivid and precise visual image, begin to make its way down the stairs in a succession of miniature waterfalls.

She continued to wash, and to sing, endlessly, while the water, which had settled into a groove in the floor that suggested long, and even weary, familiarity with its route, was disappearing beneath the door with a force and determination that made it only a matter of time before we were interrupted by an indignant owner. And indeed I soon heard footsteps pounding wetly up the stairs and along the passage; the door was flung open without even a knock and the landlord barged in, his arms flailing and his face purple with rage. His wife hovered anxiously behind him in the doorway, avoiding the flowing water in a series of balletic sidesteps and shuffles.

The landlord splashed his way over the floor towards the alcove and wrenched back the curtain. 'Don't!' I warned him, but far too late to make any impression. He reached in and turned off the tap and there was a moment of pure silence, each of us caught in the frozen gesture of a *tableau vivant*: Miss Mason with her arms crossed over her breast, staring at the landlord; he with his left hand still on the tap, gaping open-mouthed at her; his wife balanced precariously on one foot, gazing at them both and oblivious to the water that lapped around her ankle;

I seated in the chair with my legs drawn up beneath me in the position I had adopted to keep the water at bay.

Miss Mason was the first to move. She thrust the landlord vigorously aside, so that he stumbled back against the wall, and stepped out into the room. She was, of course, completely naked, with water streaming from her hair and body, but now, instead of trying to conceal herself, she placed her hands on her hips and challenged us to look. I searched around for a towel, but there was none to be seen: doubtless the landlady had chosen today to carry out her monthly washing of the linen. I realised that I still held her dress draped over my arm, but reasoned that she would prefer to be dry before she put that on again. She herself solved the dilemma by snatching the bedspread from the bed and wrapping it around her.

To my astonishment, the landlord was provoked into violent and unexpected activity by this action. Perhaps he feared that his property was about to be damaged or even impounded, or he might simply have been actuated by an atavistic and involuntary impulse to defend his possessions at all costs; at any rate, he leapt forward and started to haul the cover away from her. She resisted fiercely, holding on to her end and screaming insults at him; a brief tug-of-war took place until the landlady, who perhaps interpreted her husband's motives differently from myself, intervened and forced him to release his grip. She pinned him back against the wall like a gigantic squashed cockroach and spoke to him urgently and rapidly in a low voice. His body suddenly relaxed, his eyes glazed, and he slumped forward into her arms.

She turned her head towards me, still propping him, and explained apologetically that her husband was a very shy and modest man, who was unused to excitement of this kind. In all their years of marriage he had never –

and she lowered her eyes chastely at this point – so much as seen her naked; I could therefore well imagine the shock to his sensibilities that my 'friend's' unexpected appearance had caused. To give me only one example of his unparalleled delicacy, it was a fact that he insisted on locking the bathroom door every time he went to the toilet, even when the house was completely empty, and he would always take care to urinate in such a manner that not the slightest tinkle or splash could be heard.

Miss Mason, meanwhile, had been drying herself in a series of abstracted pats at random areas of her body, while she listened to our conversation. Now she announced that she intended to get dressed once more and would we all please leave the room. I helped the landlady with her still comatose husband and together, with some difficulty, we manoeuvred him down the stairs. She placed him in the chair behind the desk and fanned him briefly with her handkerchief. When he made no response to this, she turned her back on him and leaned across the desk towards me, propped on her elbows in a manner that revealed her breasts to me once more, and smiling at me invitingly.

I said that I had to return and find out what was happening upstairs, and added that I would attempt to clear up the mess as much as possible. Still smiling, she assured me dreamily that it was of no significance, and she would attend to it herself later. I knocked on my door and entered with Miss Mason's permission. She was sitting in front of the mirror combing her hair; she nodded with unexpected geniality when she caught sight of my reflection. 'Well, that's that,' she said gaily. 'I wouldn't like to be in your shoes when that creature returns to his senses. If I were you, I would start packing now.'

It suddenly occurred to me that she had planned all this in an attempt to force me to leave, and I took considerable satisfaction in assuring her that the landlady seemed totally unconcerned by the whole business, that I had ample tokens already of her goodwill, and that I trusted implicitly in her ability to control and direct her blustering but ineffectual husband in whatever direction she chose.

Miss Mason shrugged. She patted some strands of her still damp hair into place and turned round to face me. 'Don't trust her too much,' she warned, her tone light on the surface but with an undercurrent of intensity beneath. 'These people have their own ways of taking revenge and, as you know, they don't pay much attention to judicial process here.'

I was determined not to let her influence me and decided to change the subject. I stooped to pick up the dark cloth, which continued to cover the mirror whenever I was not using it, and which she must have discarded earlier. I draped it over the glass, half-expecting her to offer a spuriously innocent enquiry as to its purpose, but she chose not to insult my intelligence with another pretence at naïveté. 'A widespread superstition,' she mused. 'You find it in almost all cultures, at all periods. The snatching of souls by means of a mirror, distortions of personality . . .' She fell silent, staring at the uneven surface of the dressing-table and trailing her fingers through the layer of dust there. 'I must go now,' she said, standing up abruptly. 'You had better escort me through the village.'

The landlord was still slumped in his chair, snoring noisily, when we passed through the foyer; his wife was nowhere to be seen. We stepped out into the late afternoon sunlight, less harsh and dazzling than earlier, with a refreshing breeze blowing in from the sea. We were about to turn left, to retrace the route by which we had entered the village, when some half-dozen youths rushed past us, heading in the opposite direction, towards the square, almost bowling us over as they went. We looked after them and realised that practically the whole population of the village had gathered there, forming a ring around the basin and gazing in profound silence at some activity taking place towards the centre but totally concealed from our sight. Without saying a word to me, Miss Mason set off briskly towards the square, leaving me little choice but to follow her.

As soon as she reached the fountain, and in sharp contradiction to her apparent qualms about displaying herself too prominently among the villagers, Miss Mason began to edge her way through the crowd, clasping her hands before her chest and flapping her elbows in slow, rhythmic, wing-like beats that drove those on either side of her inexorably apart, as the prow of a ship diverts the waves. Some made way for her with reasonably good grace; some muttered indignantly but yielded nonetheless; a few attempted to resist and stand their ground but were driven aside by a process that employed no overt force yet which they seemed powerless to oppose. After a moment's hesitation, I followed in her wake, entering the gap she had opened up before it had time to close and reform once more.

We reached the very front of the crowd, where the waist-high wall that enclosed the fountain and kept in the water was almost hidden from sight by the press of bodies. Indeed the force exerted on me from behind, as those to the rear continued to manoeuvre for a better view, was uncomfortably strong: my thighs were rubbed quite painfully against the rough stone of the wall and I found it impossible to stand upright and was obliged to lean forward over the water at a bizarre and acutely inconvenient angle.

The murky green water lapped against the stone less than a foot from my eyes but, by twisting my neck upwards, I could see, diagonally opposite me, at the far side of the fountain, a group of children and their parents. The youngsters were all around six or seven years old; their faces were wrinkled with strain and anguish and many were sobbing quietly. They attempted to keep as far back from the wall as possible, huddling against their parents' legs, in some cases clinging to them tightly and wailing. The adults, with varying degrees of roughness and determination, were striving to disengage them and push them forward again, towards the wall.

As I watched, and on a signal from one of the villagers who seemed to be supervising the whole operation, one father seized his child firmly under the arms and deposited him on top of the wall. His face red with terror, the boy wriggled and twisted, but the man held on to him tightly, waiting for another signal. When this came he swung the boy sharply a good three feet away from the wall, so that he landed with a splash on the surface of the water, facing the statue and about ten feet away from it. Then he released his grip, leaving the child to flounder helplessly on the water.

To my amazement, instead of sinking, the boy remained upright, with the soles of his feet only an inch or two beneath the surface. He seemed as astonished at this as I was, but, gulping back his tears, he risked a tentative step forward with his right foot, his parents behind him, meanwhile, urging him on with words of endearment and encouragement. When the water supported him here too, he took heart and scampered quickly across the intervening distance to collapse at the foot of the statue, clinging to one of the shapeless lumps of stone that, if I remembered correctly, had represented a dog in the photograph of the original that I had seen.

There was a murmur of relief from the spectators and a scattering of applause. The child waved proudly to his beaming parents, who lowered their eyes and accepted the congratulations of the bystanders with modest pride. Someone pushed a little red rubber raft out from the edge of the fountain and directed it towards the centre with a large staff that resembled a boathook, but with a wooden hook on the end rather than a metal one. The child clambered unsteadily on board and was hauled briskly to shore. His parents embraced him warmly, tears of joy in their eyes.

It was the turn of another child, a girl this time. She must have been encouraged by her predecessor's success, for she made no protest at being placed on the water and, when her mother released her, she skipped lightly and fearlessly over to the statue. The applause was louder this time and an unmistakable sense of relaxation replaced the earlier tension in the crowd. The girl was brought back to her parents and a boy took her place. He too began confidently enough but, after a few paces, hesitated, panicked, and began to sink. Immediately the boat hook was stretched out towards him and he was hauled unceremoniously to the edge. He was handed over, weeping, to his shamefaced parents, who immediately dragged him away with them, the father berating him fiercely in a low voice and occasionally cuffing him on the ear for added emphasis.

The remaining children, about a dozen in all, took their turn. About half of them were successful, some advancing slowly and confidently to their goal; some moving with rapid grace and unconcern; others obviously ill at ease yet, inspired either by their parents or by an inner orientation of their own, struggling doggedly, in one case knee-deep in water by the end, towards the refuge of the statue. Those who failed, usually did so at once, either sinking immediately, uttering small cries of despair, or, after an eternity of immobility, risking a step and floundering inexorably downwards. They were ignominiously bundled off by their parents, usually to the accompaniment of a degree of violence that horrified me, for my earlier experience of the villagers had convinced me that they treated their children with exceptional gentleness and consideration.

Finally it was all over, the pressure behind and around me relaxed, and the crowd drifted off to attend to other business. I straightened up painfully, hardly able to move my neck at first; I rubbed it with my right hand, while my left sought to ease the ache in the small of my back. 'What was that all about?' I asked Miss Mason, who was by now the only other person left at the fountain. 'And it must be a delusion, isn't it? They can't really have *walked* to that statue.' I was ready enough to doubt the evidence of my senses for, owing to the acutely inconvenient angle from which I had watched the scene, and the consequent pressure of blood against my eyeballs, I had experienced something close to a blackout at different stages of the ceremony.

She muttered something that sounded like, '*Autres pays, autres moeurs*,' and gazed around as if searching for someone. The square was totally deserted now and the sun was low in the sky. 'Shall I see you back home?' I offered, hoping that, if she agreed, I might be invited to enter the Institute and perhaps even be asked to eat there and stay overnight. She shook her head: 'No, it isn't necessary now.' She began to walk towards the hotel and, when we reached it, she stopped and offered me her hand in an unexpectedly formal manner. Her grip was firm and businesslike; there was no possibility of mistaking her intention and, when I tried to keep her hand in mine a moment longer, she withdrew it with a decisive gesture.

'Shall I see you again?' I asked and, attempting a lighthearted tone, I added, 'I've no intention of leaving just yet, you know.'

She appeared not to hear me and was still staring around vaguely and expectantly. The streets were completely empty, for it was the time of the evening meal, and I fancied I could even hear the scrape of forks against plates, the rattle of cutlery, the popping of wine corks, the gulp and swallow of satisfied repletion. 'That's your decision,' she murmured, not looking at me. 'I hope you won't regret it.'

'How can I get in touch with you, at least?' I persisted. 'I may need your advice or your help.'

'You can always send a message with Ellicott,' she told me. 'He acts as our contact with the villagers. He says he knows you. He says he was once at school with you.'

With this, she walked off down the street, without a word of farewell, and without looking back at me. 'Which Ellicott?' I demanded plaintively. 'There are several of them here.' She could not have heard me or, if she did, she gave no sign. She was walking directly into the globe of the setting sun, which hovered on the horizon; the red disc circled her small black head like a gigantic halo. I was forced to blink in the intensity of the light and, when I opened my eyes once more, she had vanished.

I was not prepared to give up so easily, however, and I spent the evening considering other possible approaches that I might adopt. The landlord had gone from the chair behind the desk and when I asked his wife, as she served me my dinner of grilled red mullet, if he had recovered from his attack, she glanced at me in surprise and said there had been nothing wrong with him. My room had been thoroughly cleaned up and there was no sign of the afternoon's devastation; it was, in fact, far more wholesome than at any period since I had lived in it, and I stood for some time at the open window, leaning on the sill and enjoying the refreshing coolness of the evening air.

The window overlooked the sea and, in the quickly gathering darkness, I made out the last stragglers among the fishing boats returning to shore. As each one reached the beach, one of the men would jump out and haul the prow on to the sand; the other would pick up the basket with the day's catch and hold it proudly above his head, arms fully extended, as if displaying it for public approval. I could see no one else on the shore, however, though possibly the gesture was intended for the villagers setting up the nets to catch the souls in their nocturnal wanderings: the area where this took place was concealed from view by a curve in the coastline and a large clump of trees to my right.

The sounds from the beach faded as night asserted itself and finally I could hear nothing except the lap of waves to the shore and, somewhere within the village itself, a female voice singing softly to the accompaniment of a guitar. I would try again, I thought, making my way up to the Institute and hoping to encounter someone more forthcoming than Miss Mason. Another woman, perhaps, more open to what little charm and flattery I could offer her, or a man who would respond to a direct request for information with unambiguous co-operation or refusal. It occurred to me to follow up the woman's suggestion that I negotiate an entry by means of Ellicott, but I could not now be certain even of recognising him again or of knowing which of the many people who might bear that name she intended.

Just as I was about to draw my head inside, for the air was colder now and I was ready for bed, I heard the faint puttering of an outboard motor. I assumed that it was a particularly belated fisherman and scanned the sea for some sign of a boat; I could see nothing and was about to give up the search when I became aware that something was coming into view from behind the clump of trees and heading *away* from the shore and towards the island. I strained to make out how many people were in the boat: there were certainly two at least, but, in the rapidly intensifying darkness, I could not distinguish them or even make out if there were others. A lamp burned in the prow of the boat and soon that was all that could be seen: the vessel itself merged with the dark waters beneath it, solid, metallic layers of blackness on which the moonlight laid its fitful, erratic, barely discernible gleam.

The path to the Institute was steeper than I had expected and I was quite out of breath by the time I reached the gate. This was firmly locked and guarded at the top by an array of vicious-looking spikes; the wall which completely encircled the accessible area of the grounds was likewise defended with broken glass and sharp fragments of rusty metal. A bell dangled from a rope on the right hand side of the gate, but I hesitated to ring it and announce my presence so soon; I thought I would follow the wall round as far as I could and see what I discovered.

When I had gone about fifty yards I heard a faint ringing sound, as of metal chipping against stone. I rounded a curve of the wall and found myself almost at the edge of a cliff that dropped sheer to the sea some hundred feet below. The wall ended as it reached the cliff, and, just beside it, a man was working on some kind of statue about eight feet high and still in such an unfinished state that it was impossible to decipher what it was intended to represent. He looked up when he heard me coming, greeted me cordially and without surprise, and returned to his work.

I stood beside him for some moments, watching. He was a large, bulky man, dressed in shapeless, ill-fitting clothes, a somewhat stained light-blue shirt and brown, baggy trousers. At first he gave the appearance of being grossly overweight; then one realised that his bulk was evenly and solidly distributed, that nothing was in fact superfluous. His face too was large, but cleanly-lined and far from flabby; his hair, of a nondescript brown colour, had receded a good distance from his forehead already and clung to other areas of his skull in random patches of varying width and thickness, adhering to it like mosses on a cracked and broken wall. He puffed on an exotically curved pipe as he worked, occasionally removing it from his mouth and stepping back to contemplate his progress with an air of quiet satisfaction.

I decided not to intervene and to let him make the first move towards conversation. He seemed to have forgotten me already and to be thoroughly absorbed in his work, chipping with hammer and chisel at the unevenly shaped stone base that supported the main bulk of his creation. This was made up of an extraordinary conglomeration of materials that looked as if they had been chosen and applied totally at random: I could make out leaves, twigs, and even whole branches of trees; stones, boulders, shells, and pebbles of every shape, size, and colour; fragments of metal and broken glass that glittered and shone in the sunlight; even whole pieces of cloth, netting, and canvas, that seemed to include items of clothing such as shirts and dresses as well as what must have been patches of sailcloth from the fishermen's boats. All these were held together in the most haphazard fashion, usually with little more than dabs of mud slapped on here and there, and more often simply balanced or interwoven one with another in an ingenious but decidedly unstable fashion. I expected the whole edifice to collapse with the first strong gust of wind but, though it swayed and wavered under the breeze that had blown steadily all morning, it somehow maintained its precarious equilibrium, performing an intricate dance, a pattern of to-and-fro, back-and-forth, that always returned it to its original upright stance.

'What is it?' I ventured finally, when he continued to ignore the discreet coughs, shufflings, and uneasy movements with which I had attempted to remind him of my presence. 'It's very beautiful, but what is it meant to be?'

He looked up, startled, as if he had not expected to find me still there, and removed the pipe from his mouth. 'What is it?' he repeated thoughtfully, gazing at me and nodding his head several times. 'Can't you see that it's a copy of the statue in the village square?'

I thought that he was joking and was about to laugh in amused sympathy with his jest when I realised that the expression on his face was totally serious. I changed the laugh into a cough and, cocking my head to one side, examined his creation intently. 'Well . . .' I mused, 'I wouldn't have thought so at first, but now that you mention it. . . . Yes, I can definitely make out the wolf here, and this must be a spear, I suppose, and this, yes, this must be one of the dogs.'

'Wolf? Spear? Dog?' he repeated in amazement. 'What on earth are you talking about?'

'The statue in the village,' I stammered. 'It represents a wolf hunt, doesn't it?'

'Who told you that?'

I explained that I had seen it on one of the Seahorse cards, though I admitted that my personal observation of the statue would never have led me to give it that particular interpretation.

'So they call it a Wolf Hunt now?' he remarked mysteriously, more to himself than to me. 'That's an interesting development indeed.' Then, addressing himself to me, he continued: 'The original statue had nothing to do with wolf hunts at all. It represented a local saint or martyr, a regional variant of St Sebastian I suppose, transfixed by arrows. Of course it's so damaged and weathered now that you can't make that out very easily, but if you examine it carefully you'll see that I'm right. But a Wolf Hunt . . .' he continued, forgetting me once more, 'that is really interesting. I must tell the others about it at lunch.'

I looked closely at his own construction again, trying to interpret it in the light of what he had just told me but, search as I might, I could not distinguish anything that reminded me of a human figure or any kind of human activity. It was merely a bizarre confusion of shapes and colours, some, especially when viewed from a certain angle or with the light falling on them from a certain direction, attractive and intriguing enough and occasionally even seeming on the point of suggesting an association or meaning of some kind that, with the constant realignment caused by the tremors and puffs of wind all around, was almost immediately distorted and lost.

I wondered whether he expected me to offer a detailed

comment on his creation, but he had replaced his pipe in his mouth and resumed his task. He was steadily chipping away at the base of the statue in a manner that would inevitably erode the foundation and render its balance even more fragile than before. I held my peace about the dangers of this, however, assuming that he must have some reason for what he was doing, and instead offered him my name and asked for his own.

'Yes, I've heard all about you from Maria,' he grunted, his pipe still clenched in his teeth. 'I gather you had quite an exciting time together yesterday.'

I was uncertain how to follow this up and instead repeated my request for his name: 'And you,' I suggested tentatively, 'you're not Dr Daniels, are you?'

He straightened up and smiled at me. 'Goodness, no,' he said, a boyish grin on his face. 'He's far older and wiser than I. My name is Davers. David Davers, Dave Davers, Davy Davers, spelt with a "y", "ey", or "ie", take your choice. I've been called all of them in my time. Even Daft Davy,' he added in a thoughtful tone of voice. I stretched out my hand, but he had turned back to his statue and was regarding it critically, his chin propped in his hand. 'That'll do for today, I think,' he reflected. 'Mustn't get carried away and try for too much at once. Anyway,' he consulted his watch, 'it's lunch time.'

I hoped, and indeed half-expected, that he would invite me in to join them, but instead he offered me his hand and said goodbye. 'Pleased to meet you,' he assured me. 'I'll tell Maria you were here. She'll be sorry to have missed you.' He turned his back to me, dismissing me solidly from his attention, and contemplated his work once more.

I hesitated a moment, then turned to leave. After a few yards, and just before the curve of the wall would hide him from my view, I looked back at him once more. At that moment a particularly strong gust of wind caught the statue, making it sway alarmingly, but doing no greater damage than to snatch away a stray piece of cloth that danced and hovered tantalisingly a foot from the very edge of the cliff before being seized once more and dashed away out of sight. I expected Davers to show some concern over this, even to make some attempt to retrieve it before it was too late, but he remained immobile, standing with folded arms and gazing on impassively. A blue curl of smoke rose from his pipe; it too floated a moment in the air before dissolving as though it had never been.

'Wolf Hunts and Saint Sebastians,' I mused, as I strolled back down the path. 'I wonder if everyone in the village has his own explanation of the statue.' I remembered the picture I had seen on the Seahorse card, that had so much resembled a photograph, and which, if it was in any way authentic, would presumably give the lie to Davers' claim. I should have mentioned it to him, I reproached myself, that would have settled the matter; but, despite his dishevelled appearance, the man had an air of quiet authority that had silenced me and, it now seemed, had made it actually impossible for me to think of any objections to his statements while I was still in his presence.

In any case, I realised, he would simply have pointed out that no photograph claiming to reproduce the original condition of the statue could possibly be authentic. It now occurred to me that, despite the photographic texture of the Seahorse cards, I had never seen anyone in the village using or carrying a camera, and I could remember no shops that sold photographic equipment or even rolls of film. I determined to check this as soon as I reached the village and I quickened my pace, uncomfortably aware as I did so that the sun had reached its peak and that I was hungry and thirsty, as well as hot and footsore.

The main street of the village was deserted, the inhabitants having retired indoors for their midday meal and the inevitable siesta that followed it. I walked slowly along, checking the grimy windows of the half-dozen shops: the fishmonger, the baker, the grocer, the shop that sold a nondescript assortment of clothes and boots, the one that seemed to account for everything else – fishing gear, candles and oil-lamps, furniture, tools, household supplies. I saw nothing resembling a camera in any of them, and I was about to give up the search when I remembered that I had not been aware of the butcher's before Maria had taken me there and that there might be similar shops hidden away in the three or four alleys that branched off from the main street and completed the whole topography of the village.

I explored first the street where the butcher's – closed as before and looking even less prepossessing and attractive than yesterday – was situated, but the buildings surrounding it were all houses. I thought I heard a forlorn chirping from inside as I passed and speeded up in a vain attempt to outpace my conscience. The street along from it was likewise made up entirely of dwellings, but, crossing the main road once more and beginning on the other side, I discovered, in a cul-de-sac even darker and gloomier than the one where the butcher's was secreted, a tiny shop that, in other surroundings, would have been considered a general store.

The door was locked and the windows were thick with dirt and dust. Visibility was made even more difficult by the fact that the owner (or his predecessor) had once scrawled a list of special offers and prices in a now faded white paint that was already peeling with age but still obscured most of the area of the glass through which it might have been possible to peer. Nevertheless, by scrubbing furiously with my sleeve, I was able to clear an area about a foot square through which I hoped I might obtain a general view of the interior.

Whether by sheer chance or not, however, I found I had exposed a photograph that had been stuck directly on to the pane, from the inside, exactly at eye level. It was dingy and fly-specked, curled and yellow with age, and it took several minutes for me to realise what it represented. My slowness could also be accounted for by an instinctive refusal to accept the evidence of my senses, for the picture, as, finally, I was forced to admit to myself, was of nothing other than the landlord and Miss Mason, in my hotel room, standing facing each other in the shower compartment, in the position I have already minutely described – he with his hand on the tap, she with her arms crossed over her breasts to shield them.

I closed my eyes and shook my head violently in disbelief. I examined the photo again: faded and decrepit as it was, there could be no doubt about the subject; Maria was face-on to the camera and the landlord, though he was visible only in profile, was equally unmistakable. The whole thing, though, was unthinkable, impossible: there was no one present at the scene who could possibly have taken a photograph, and the patina of age on the image, the obvious wear and tear it had suffered, made it unlikely that it could have been taken only the previous day. I tried to visualise exactly how we had all stood and to see if perhaps the landlady, unknown to me, could have taken a photograph; but I remembered that I had scanned the scene carefully, noting each detail, and I knew that she could not have been responsible.

It could only be a hoax, I realised, something concocted between Miss Mason and the landlord, for reasons best known to themselves, and designed to baffle and confuse me. Perhaps they intended to frighten me, to make me doubt the reliability of my senses, and so induce me to leave the village. Miss Mason, I remembered, had seemed particularly anxious to see me go. But then, how could they have anticipated that I would stumble across this neglected and out-of-the-way shop window; how could they have known that I would clear exactly this particular space?

I pulled myself together and strode to the shop door, which was firmly secured with a huge padlock. I hammered on it loudly with my fist, determined to get at the truth of this matter and, for the moment at least, oblivious to any thoughts of how my behaviour would appear to others, or might be interpreted by them. There was no sound from inside, no response, and, in my growing rage and frustration, I began to beat on the door with both fists and even to kick it in a gesture of futile rage. I heard the grating sound above me of shutters being opened; they crashed back against the stone wall and a woman's indignant voice demanded to know what was happening.

I stepped a couple of paces back into the street (taking myself almost to the other side in the process) and craned my head back to look upwards. I found that I was staring directly into the sun that, perversely, was visible only from that particular angle in the street; I shielded my eyes with my hands but the after-image still dazzled and blinded me. 'Where is the owner of this shop?' I demanded. 'I have to speak to him.'

'The owner?' she repeated. 'What owner? The shop has been closed for months now, perhaps years. Mr Maurett died . . .' and she trailed off into a senile clucking and muttering, attempting to work out the exact date of the man's death by a process of recounting every noteworthy incident that had occurred in the past decade to herself and all the members of her numerous family.

I left her in the midst of this and set off back to the hotel. Even if what she said was true, it was still possible that the conspirators might have obtained access to the shop and set their trap for me, though the futility and improbability of this, the minute and almost negligible likelihood of my ever coming across it, made this virtually impossible to accept. But why was I thinking this, I wondered, when I *had* in fact come across it, whatever the odds against my being expected to do so? The whole thing was beyond me and I felt that I needed a rest and a drink to clear my head.

I passed the tavern and sat down at one of the sidewalk tables. The landlord noticed me at once and came bustling towards me, beaming cheerfully. 'Welcome, Mr Everrich, welcome,' he effused. 'You are a stranger from us for too long.' I felt like seizing the grimy collar of his soiled shirt and shaking the truth out of him come what may, but I resisted the impulse. I ordered a glass of wine and observed the other customers. As usual, a game of Seahorse was taking place nearby, but, though I thought I recognised some of the players, no one, to my relief, suggested that I take part this time.

As I sipped my wine and idly watched the activity around me, I realised that it would be easy for me to check whether my suspicions about collusion between Miss Mason and the landlord were true. I stood up and wandered over to the nearest table, where I positioned myself behind one of the players as if I were mildly interested in learning more about the game and how to play it. He glanced up at me with a frown when he became aware of my presence, but then seemed to accept it and returned his attention to the game.

The cards flew on to the table, were shuffled and re-distributed at such a pace, that I found it difficult to identify clearly the images on those that passed through his hands. Some, that I had never seen before, roused brief and disturbing stabs of recognition but, as I was searching for one image in particular, I tried to ignore these and refused to allow them to distract me. If, I thought, I discovered that a card showing Maria Mason and the landlord together in the shower had recently been added to the pack (for, whatever other mysteries the game contained, it was clear that the subjects could shift from time to time and were in some way tied in with the daily activities of the villagers), then this would confirm that some kind of net, for whatever reason, was being woven around me.

The man behind whom I was standing finished his share in the game with a great flourish, spilling counters lavishly over the table top and uttering a blood-curdling yell of triumph as he did so. He scraped his chair sharply backwards, catching me unawares and dealing me a painful blow on the shin. 'I go pee now,' he told me. 'You take my place.' Before I could protest, he had pushed me firmly into his chair and, within another moment, I had a full set of cards before me.

I picked them up and examined them cautiously. The first two were familiar: *Black Dog* and *Mermaid*. The third was an example of cheap pornography from which I automatically averted my eyes in instinctive disgust; I forced myself to return to it nonetheless out of pure scientific detachment. A man and a woman, their faces turned away from the camera, were copulating in the manner of dogs, crouched on all fours, the man's erect organ clearly visible as it penetrated his partner from behind. Despite the anonymity of the figures, something about the droop of the woman's breasts reminded me of the landlady, though it was impossible to confirm this suspicion from any other evidence. The fourth card, taken at night with a flashbulb, was ambiguous and virtually indecipherable: it seemed, as far as I could make out, to represent a wall or a cliff or a hill, with some unidentifiable object hurtling downwards from the top; what might be a human head, but might equally be merely a tuft of grass or a large rock, peered anxiously over the edge.

It was the fifth card, however, which caught and transfixed my attention, rendering me oblivious to the nudges and exhortations of the other players, the complaints that greeted my refusal to participate in the game. For it was a photograph of the statue taken, apparently, like the first one I had seen, at a time when it was still brand-new yet with the contemporary aspect of the village forming a background. Only this time, instead of representing a Wolf Hunt, the statue showed a human figure bound to a slender column, its head thrown back in the final throes of agony, the mouth open in a soundless howl of pain, the body pierced, from every angle and with every ingenious variety of imaginative cruelty, by dozens of arrows. Arrows that had rammed right through the body, from front to back or the reverse, steel tip and goose feather visible, the shaft gouging unseen through flesh and gut. Arrows that had banged against a barrier of bone and snapped off short with the impact. Arrows that had, with perhaps deliberate refinement, merely pierced a corner of the skin, pinning two folds of flesh together like a piece of needlework set aside to receive further attention later. Two arrows crosswise through the neck.

One arrow, horribly, through an eye, the shaft pointing directly upwards, to the indifferent sky, as the dying head jerked backwards.

I found that my lips were dry and I had to moisten them repeatedly with my tongue before I could speak. 'This card,' I stammered, 'where did it come from? What is it?' I stretched out my hand, displaying the picture to the other players. '*Martyr*, of course,' one of them told me impatiently. 'It has always been there. You have seen the statue, haven't you?'

'No, it isn't,' I remonstrated, my mind so confused that I could scarcely articulate the words correctly. 'The statue is a Wolf Hunt. You all told me so. There was a card of a Wolf Hunt when I last played.'

They stared at me in silence.

'But surely!' I shouted, unnerved by their lack of response. 'Look, I'll show you.' I seized the cards that lay on the table and rummaged through them, spilling some on the floor in my haste. There was none representing a Wolf Hunt. I stood up and almost ran round the table, grabbing the cards held by the other players, glancing at them and tossing them aside. No Wolf Hunt. I stood glaring at them, looking, no doubt, a ridiculous enough sight, with my hair flopping damply forward on my forehead, my face flushed, my mouth open. 'Where is Hanslett?' I demanded. 'Hanslett showed me the card of the Wolf Hunt. He told me all about it.'

'Which Hanslett?' one of the players asked me calmly. 'There are many Hansletts here. You must tell us which one you mean.'

I could take it no longer. I turned and ran from the table, knocking over chairs, and perhaps even those sitting on them, as I went. As I left the shade of the tattered awning that shielded the outdoors section of the tavern from the worst glare of the sun, the heat struck me like a blow in the face. I staggered, but shook off the proffered assistance of a passer-by, and tottered weakly back to the hotel.

I must have collapsed on my bed and fallen into a profound sleep as soon as I reached my room. When I awoke, it was night and a breeze streamed with refreshing coolness through the still-open window. I was ravenously hungry, having eaten nothing since breakfast, but in all other respects felt restored to something like my normal self. I glanced automatically at my wrist to check the time before remembering what had happened to my watch; from the silence within the hotel and from the surroundings generally, I deduced that it must be at least midnight. I thought that I would take a walk, perhaps up to the Institute once more, in the hope of picking up a clue that might put the bewildering events of the past two days into some intelligible perspective.

The street was deserted when I stepped out into it, and bathed in the serene radiance of an almost full moon. No lights were visible in any of the houses and I moved as quietly and cautiously as possible, anxious to avoid creating a disturbance. A dog barked restlessly in the distance and I fancied idly that it might be my old antagonist, scenting my presence from afar off and warning me not to meddle with him again. I would be travelling in the opposite direction from him, however, and could consider myself safe enough for the time being. When I passed the church, whose bizarrely ornamented pinnacles were framed directly by the halo of the moon and stood out with extraordinary sharpness, as delicate and elaborate as fretwork or the subtlest lace, I realised that, for the first time since my arrival, the village seemed beautiful to me. The darkness smoothed out the flaws in the chipped and flaking stonework of the houses, the dingy paint that had been applied decades ago and never renewed. Even the squat ugliness of the buildings was softened by the shadows that lay between them, joining and merging them into an unexpected harmony, while the moonlight appeared to enhance those few features worthy of admiration and attention, such as the church itself.

I passed quietly in front of the church and then out on to the road that led up to the Institute. The air was full of tantalising scents that I failed to recognise or even properly distinguish one from another; the whole, nevertheless, filled me with a sense of serene well-being and made me feel that, whatever the frustrations and humiliations I had suffered since my arrival, I had been right to come and some solution was at hand that would give a pattern and significance to all my experiences.

The Institute loomed ahead of me, dark and forbidding, brooding on its headland as it surveyed the featureless waters beneath it. I paused. There was no point in trying to enter and I ought to be wary of possible traps and pitfalls set out for intruders. I decided to begin with the area that I knew already and work my way cautiously from there to less familiar sections. I skirted the wall, keeping close to it and touching it occasionally with my hands to reasure myself. The night was darker now, perhaps foretelling a storm, with clouds frequently obscuring the moon and its light often blocked as I moved by the intervention of the turrets and battlements of the ancient building to my side.

I rounded the final curve and saw Davers' statue before me, rocking gently in the wind and occasionally uttering a groan, a creak of complaint, as it was shifted into an unfamiliar or unpremeditated alignment. I noticed that, during the afternoon, Davers had refined the connexion of figure and base to what seemed an absurdly dangerous extent: they met at a point shaped like the stem of an hourglass, but barely thicker than my little finger, a link so fragile and insecure that it seemed the merest puff of wind, an incautious breath, should be sufficient to overturn it.

I moved closer to it, yet keeping a safe distance. The figure itself appeared to have been elaborated since my visit; new materials had been added that somehow gave it a raffish and daredevil aspect: leaves and bones; shells that glistened and glowed as if still damp from the sea; sparkling fragments of cheap costume jewellery, glimmering dull red or flashing vibrant yellow as the movements of the statue brought them into range of the moonlight; segments of rope or fishing line, tarred and frayed; a birdcage – empty, as I noted with some relief; a battered lobster pot containing pieces of shell and claw; an old 78 r.p.m. record; and the whole edifice now crowned with a rakishly poised lampshade that tipped and bobbed to its own precarious and private rhythm. The result looked even less like a Saint Sebastian than before but, as I had entertained doubts about Davers' earlier explanation of his work, this did not worry me unduly.

As I examined the statue, I became aware of the sound of an outboard motor from the area of the coast immediately below me. I dropped to my hands and knees and crawled cautiously to the edge of the cliff and peered over. A boat was heading away from the shore in the direction of the island; it lay directly in a shaft of moonlight and I saw that it contained four people, two men and two women. I recognised Davers and Miss Mason immediately; the second man, who I assumed was Dr Daniels, stood proudly at the steering wheel (for the boat was quite a large one and possessed a covered-in cabin), his massive mane of silver hair flowing around him in the breeze. It was less easy to distinguish much about the second woman, who sat curled up in the stern, but she appeared to be young and dark-haired.

The boat crossed from the rippled moonlight into the black, gently heaving water beyond and, as it did so, I heard a powerful bass voice – that of Dr Daniels, no doubt – raised in song. The tune of a familiar sea shanty, that I had first learned in school, floated across the water towards me; then it was abruptly cut off, in mid-phrase, and Daniels' booming voice switched to an admonition: 'Look at your statue there, Davy, isn't it magnificent!'

Anxious to avoid detection, I scrambled back a couple of feet and, though I have no recollection of actually touching it, or even coming at all close to it, my movements set off an unforeseen reaction in the statue, which began to sway and vibrate in a totally uncontrolled manner. Frozen with horror, I watched it, praying that it would right itself in time and debating whether to rush forward and attempt somehow to steady it. Before I could decide on a course of action, the statue solved the problem for me by starting to tip inexorably forward, towards the edge; it hung suspended for a moment and seemed almost on the point of taking a pendulum-like swing backwards, then it gathered momentum and plunged forward once more, the body parting company from the base with a sharp click.

I heard it scrape and rattle its way down the cliffside, banging itself to pieces in the process; at last there was a huge splash as it hit the water, followed by a ripple of smaller ones. I wriggled forward on my belly to take a look over the edge: a series of concentric circles spread away from the place of impact and, at the very centre,

83

some isolated objects bobbed and floated – the birdcage, the lampshade, some shreds of clothing.

Voices came to me clearly across the water from the boat: 'What the hell was that?' 'What happened?' 'Oh, David, your statue!' and then it must have been Daniels who announced, in a measured and dignified tone, like that of a judge passing sentence: 'Someone interfered with your construction, Davy. I can see him now, peering over the cliff-top.'

I crawled back out of view, trembling and apprehensive. Would they return to shore and search for me, I wondered, or would they continue with their excursion? It seemed safer not to wait to find out. I backed yet further away, until there seemed no possibility that I could still be seen from the water, and then I rose to my feet and raced back towards the path, stumbling over uneven tufts of grass and once catching my foot in a shallow depression and sprawling flat on my face. I slowed down when I reached the road and began to walk at a more normal pace, my heart thudding loudly and my chest heaving painfully to the rasping motion of my breath. The moon had vanished behind a thick bank of clouds and I shivered in the sudden coolness of the air. Everything was quiet. I wondered how Daniels and his companions would return to the Institute, whether I might even encounter them on the way; but reasoned that there must be some access from within the building to the shore, no doubt by a series of steps carved out centuries ago by the earliest owners.

A dog barked faintly in the distance and, in my state of heightened sensibility, the sound seemed to carry a note of savage triumph. I wondered if I should leave the area after all: disaster seemed to accompany all my actions, even the most innocent and well-intentioned, and the little I had discovered about the Institute and the village had served to confuse rather than enlighten me. But there is a streak of stubbornness in me that refuses to allow me to give up easily on an enterprise once undertaken, and the mysteries I had uncovered offered a perverse fascination that counterbalanced, at least to some extent, their irritating obscurities.

The dog barked again and, though it was perhaps a trick of the wind, the noise sounded distinctly closer. I quickened my pace for, though I am no coward, I had no desire to tangle, unarmed, with a vicious brute like the one that had attempted to assault me a few days ago. I fancied that the sky was becoming lighter towards the horizon; dawn was no doubt close at hand and the villagers would shortly be making their way to the shore to take down their nets, restoring to them their more mundane significance as catchers of fish in place of the exotic obligation of snaring souls. I could understand their suspicions of Daniels now and share their curiosity as to the purpose of his nocturnal visits to the island, though I still found it impossible to accept the explanations offered by the superstitious natives.

Once again the dog barked, and this time there was no mistaking its proximity. I could almost hear the pattering of its feet as it bounded across the fields towards me, its jaws wide open, the tongue lolling out, the fearsome teeth agape. Fortunately I was within sight of the village and, though I refrained from breaking into a run, I speeded up to my fastest walking pace. The silence around me seemed ominous now: I imagined the creature stalking me, keeping pace in one of the ditches that separated the road from the fields, waiting till I was off guard, waiting its opportunity to spring.

I was now about twenty yards from the nearest house

and I forced myself to slow down, to avoid any overt manifestation of fear or distress. I would not look behind me, lest I see the beast padding silently in my rear, its fangs flecked with a drool of saliva, the last gleams of moonlight glinting in its eyes. I was level with the house now and the church was only a few yards off; when I reached that, though I am far from being a believer, I felt somehow safe and I turned abruptly to confront whatever might be behind me. The road was empty, nothing lurked in its shadows, and on the horizon the first red rays of sunlight were visible. I expelled the breath that I had not known I was holding within me, and walked along the main street to the hotel. There was a light in the baker's as I passed, a bustle of activity within, and the irresistible smell of fresh bread.

I knocked on the door and waited, in the sudden silence from within, for some response. The door was creaked open a couple of inches and a woman's voice asked what I wanted. I said that I was famished, I had been out all night, and could I buy some bread. After another pause, the door was edged open enough to allow me to squeeze through, and I was invited, in a surly tone, to enter. I stood by the counter, watching the activity that was visible in the inner room: men passed to and fro, scooping up the new loaves with long-handled wooden implements, flattened at the end; or balancing heavy trays of bread on their heads as they prepared them for delivery. One of the men noticed me and nodded familiarly, though I did not recognise him; no doubt he was one of the habitual players of Seahorse. The woman brought me a loaf, almost too hot to handle, crisp and brown and fragrant. She asked me twice the normal price and I gave her all the change I carried in my pocket; she examined the coins suspiciously, then nodded in surprised satisfaction.

I stood leaning on the counter, breaking off fragments of the bread and chewing it slowly, lingering over each mouthful. The men went about their work by the ovens, silhouetted blackly against the red flames inside as they jerked open the doors; the counter vibrated and the whole shop seemed to rattle as they slammed them shut, locking the loaves inside like souls trapped for ever in the confines of a narrow Hell.

I slept long that morning and might even have spent all day in bed if I had not been wakened, sometime in mid-afternoon, by a knocking on my door. I offered no invitation to enter and merely turned over irritably, pulling the sheet over my head. I heard the door open, the sound of quick footsteps, the quiet breathing of someone standing beside my bed. I rolled back to face the door and edged myself indignantly up on one elbow.

Miss Mason was standing about a foot away from me, contemplating me thoughtfully. 'What do you want?' I asked, my gaze flicking automatically towards the shower compartment.

She laughed. 'Don't worry,' she assured me. 'I don't intend to take a shower today. I've come for another reason.' She paused. 'Can't you guess?' she asked quietly.

I shook my head. The sounds of the village came to me through the open window, the laughter of children, women gossiping, the yells and shouts from a game of Seahorse.

'No,' I said. 'I've no idea.'

She sighed. 'There was a statue. On the cliff-top, beside the Institute. Davers built it. David Davers, you know him. You talked to him. You saw the statue.'

I nodded.

Her voice was gentle, almost caressing. 'The statue

isn't there any longer. It fell into the sea. It fell into the sea last night. Someone must have pushed it.'

She paused. The silence lengthened out intolerably.

'Have you any idea who might have pushed it?'

I shook my head. My mouth was dry and I slipped my tongue out furtively to moisten it. 'One of the villagers, perhaps?' I suggested, my voice cracking as I spoke. I deepened it. 'A child, or someone out for a stroll.' Inspiration seized me. 'Why don't you ask Ellicott? He'd know, if anyone would.'

A frown creased her forehead. 'Ellicott?' she repeated sharply. 'What has Ellicott got to do with it? Which Ellicott do you mean?'

'Never mind,' I mumbled. 'It must have been a child, then.'

She shook her head. 'It happened last night, after midnight. No child would dare go near the Institute at that time. We have,' she smiled faintly, 'a bad reputation with the local children, for some reason. Totally unmerited, of course. No, it wasn't a child. You see, we had all gone to bed, but my window overlooks the area where the statue is – where it was. I was awakened by a splash, and when I looked out of the window I saw a man, bent almost double, running away. He was far too large to be a child.'

I wondered, not merely why she was lying, but why, when she obviously suspected me and must have known that I had seen them in the boat, she should even bother with the elaborate deception. I decided to test her in return. 'Pity you didn't have a camera,' I commiserated. 'Then you could have photographed him and solved your problem.'

'You don't need a camera to take photographs,' she remarked, strangely.

'What do you mean?'

She shrugged. 'Something I read somewhere. People in Russia, I think it was, who can produce photographic images mentally, without a camera, without film.' She fell silent. 'None of this is really the point,' she went on suddenly. 'I came here to say that David can't undertake the task of building the statue again. He's far too busy for one thing, also he's heartbroken at what happened to it. He put so much of himself into it and now it's all gone. He's quite prostrate, I assure you.'

This information fitted oddly with the mental image of Davers that I had created for myself, but I decided not to contest it. I waited for her to continue.

'We *need* that statue,' she brought out urgently, 'I can't tell you why, not just at the moment, but we need it. That's why – ' she paused, unexpectedly at a loss for words, her habitual assurance and self-confidence apparently gone. 'That's why we need you,' she pleaded. 'To build us another one.'

I was not taken in for a moment by any of this. I remembered her earlier manipulations, the hand on my arm, the caress, then the overruling, the trampling down of my protests when it suited her. 'Why do you ask me? I'm no sculptor.'

She moved closer to me. She put her hand on my arm once more. 'Neither is David. But you don't need to be. We're not looking for an artistic masterpiece, that's not the purpose of it. And I thought of you because – ' I expected her to flutter her eyelashes coyly at me at this point, perhaps to lay her head on my shoulder and whisper that she thought of me because she had come to *admire* and *respect* me so much, perhaps even, dropping her voice even further and blushing, to *love* me. If she had attempted any of this I would have pushed her away in disgust and refused utterly to co-operate. Perhaps she sensed this, or, more likely, she was far too intelligent to resort to anything so crude in any case. 'Because,' she went on, 'you seem to have plenty of spare time and you seem a pleasant and competent enough person. You're here as a tourist, aren't you? That's what you told me.'

I doubted I had said anything even as specific as that to her, but it seemed the easiest explanation to offer. 'I'm a sort of writer too,' I confessed, spurred unaccountably to a degree of honesty by the situation and prompted, perhaps, by a sense of guilt at my deception over the statue. 'I'm working on a book.'

'On remote, isolated peoples and their customs?' she suggested.

I agreed that that was exactly the subject.

'Well, you'll still have plenty of time for that too. Will you start tomorrow?'

I nodded.

'We'll expect you early, then. Say, nine o'clock?'

I nodded again. She stood up and smoothed her dress down primly. 'It's so nice of you to help us,' she said. She flashed me a warm, dazzling smile, and disappeared through the door.

I reached the Institute shortly before nine o'clock and rang the bell by the gate. Through the bars I saw the large oak door, with its ancient metal studs, open, and Maria came along the gravel path towards me. I expected her to invite me inside but, after greeting me, she led me along the side of the wall to the spot where the statue used to stand. Piled around its base was a heap of materials similar to those originally employed by Davers; I noticed, to my surprise, that the bird cage, the lampshade, and the lobster pot had been retrieved from the ocean and had been restored, none the worse for wear, to take their place in my new construction. I picked up the lobster pot and studied it carefully: there was no way of telling if it really was the one in which the two lobsters had massacred each other, though I suspected that it was; the owner had at one time painted his name on it, but the letters had faded with exposure to the elements and only the ending of the word, '-ETT', was visible. If this *was* the same pot, however, it would confirm my belief that the man who had lured me into his boat was certainly not called Ellicott.

Since our conversation the day before, I had hardened my attitude towards Maria; I felt she had won too easy a victory over me and that I had a right to know more about what I was supposed to be doing and why. 'Before I start on this,' I told her firmly, 'I want to know what it's supposed to represent and why you people want to build it. After all,' I went on more hesitantly, disconcerted by her calm, expressionless response, 'I can't be expected to create without knowing what I'm creating.' I giggled in mild embarrassment.

'But surely David told you? It's a copy of the statue down there in the village. It doesn't really matter what it looks like eventually, for the statue itself is completely shapeless. No one has any idea what it was originally intended to represent. Of course, there are all kinds of theories . . .' Her gaze wandered away from me to scan the cloudless sky, the white-capped sea below us. 'Do what you like with it,' she urged me. 'Use your imagination. No one will ever know the difference.'

'But why are you building it?' I persisted.

'A gesture.' She waved her hand vaguely towards the ocean. A gull flew past, level with the top of the cliff, and screeched harshly. 'Some recompense for our presence here. Returning thanks for their co-operation.' She was silent once more. 'We're leaving here soon,' she concluded, unexpectedly. 'Perhaps a week, perhaps less. You don't have much time.'

She turned, as usual without a formal farewell, and set off towards the gate. Her loose, flowered cotton dress swayed as she walked, flapping against her calves. Though sturdy, her legs were well shaped; her whole body was neat and trim. I sighed, and turned to my task.

The morning passed quickly and even pleasantly, once I had settled to my work and had begun to take an interest in it. As the sun rose higher in the sky, I took off my shirt and worked bare to the waist; sweat occasionally trickled down the back of my neck and between my shoulder-blades, but the sensation was not an unpleasant one. I began to find a certain fascination in choosing from among the materials available to me, selecting an artistically satisfactory combination, and – the most difficult task of all – weaving these into a harmony that would remain both flexible and stable, alert to the movements of the atmosphere and yet with its own inner strength and integrity. I had one or two early disasters, when I risked something too elaborate and complex without providing the proper foundation; I quickly learned to move more slowly and patiently, however, and, by noon, had laid down the groundwork at least for something of which I could feel legitimately proud.

Maria brought me out some lunch, an attractive selection of cold meats, pâté, fresh bread, olives, cheese, and fruit (including my own personal and rarely tasted favourite, fresh figs). Everything was beautifully, even artistically, laid out on a large platter, with colours, shapes, and textures so ingeniously and tastefully combined or juxtaposed that I hesitated to disturb their harmony by actually eating anything. I invited her to join me, but she shook her head and said she had already eaten; she sat down beside me on the grass nevertheless, crossing her legs and smoothing her dress over her knees.

I marvelled where she had obtained meat of such quality and said that I had never been offered cheese at the hotel. 'Oh, it's easy enough,' she said vaguely. 'When you get to know the shopkeepers.' I doubted whether the butcher we had visited could ever supply anything as fine as this, but decided this was no time to risk straining relations by asking awkward questions. I ate in silence for some time, gazing out to sea. The sun sparkled on the water, which ran through a gamut of shades between the extremes of sky-blue and leaf-green, the colours in between shifting by such imperceptible degrees, each subtly merging and blending with its companion, that, strain as I might, I could finally make out nothing except an undifferentiated mass of greenish-blue.

Meanwhile I was steadily clearing my plate and discovered, as I did so, that the dish itself was painted in an elaborate and exquisite design of flowers and birds, gorgeously coloured, with each detail sharply and precisely observed. I asked Maria where it had come from: 'The villagers used to make them,' she told me, 'decades, even centuries ago. Very few of them survive, they break easily and no one seemed to value them very much or to care about preserving them. They've lost the secret of it now, there are no artists or craftsmen left any longer.'

I nodded, remembering the shapeless masses of hardened clay from which I ate my meals in the hotel, the crude glassware from which I drank my wine. I wiped the plate clean with a tuft of grass and examined it more closely. The colours glowed as freshly as if they had been painted yesterday and I felt a stab of doubt at Maria's claim that the dishes were hundreds of years old. 'Why did you serve me food on something as precious as this?' I asked suspiciously. 'Suppose it were to be broken?'

She laughed softly. 'I know I can trust you,' she assured me. 'You're not the type to break things, to bump into them, to knock them over.'

I felt that she was mocking me and handed the plate back to her. 'I'd better get on with my work,' I said, struggling to my feet. One of my legs had gone numb beneath me and I had to massage it for a few moments, grunting with pain. 'How long do you want me to stay for?'

'It's up to you. I'll insist only on the mornings. After lunch you can stay or leave, you can do what you like.'

I offered to stay for an hour or two longer, as my task was just becoming interesting. She said that, in that case, she would see me the following morning and, before leaving, she examined carefully what I had achieved so far, walking round it and considering it from every angle. She nodded approvingly once or twice, though she said nothing. Then she set off back for the Institute, as usual without a word of goodbye.

I worked on steadily for another hour, becoming increasingly satisfied with what I was doing and occasionally even beginning to take risks, to experiment with unusual combinations and daring balances, in a manner far removed from my earlier caution. Once or twice I heard the bell ringing at the Institute gate and wondered who might be visiting them. Maria had spoken of 'co-operation' from the villagers, had mentioned once that 'Ellicott' was some kind of go-between; yet Hanslett, for one, had spoken of the Institute with genuine fear, even hatred, and had not even my original Ellicott threatened to attack the building, to destroy it?

At last I came to a point where I felt my inspiration was deserting me for the day. I stepped back to contemplate my creation, falling unconsciously, as I realised with a wry grimace, into exactly the pose Davers had adopted, arms akimbo, head cocked slightly to one side, feet spread apart and my body rocking gently from heel to toe. It wanted only a pipe stuck between my teeth for the resemblance to be complete. Though there was no one to see me or to note the comparison, I quickly changed to a position with my hands on my hips instead. I felt that what I had done was good enough for the time being and stooped to pick up my shirt. I hoped I had not exposed my back too long to the sun; I had acquired something of a tan already on previous outings, but, absorbed in my work, I had left my back bare much longer than I had originally intended.

I set off towards the path and, rounding the corner, I almost collided with a man who was just coming out of the Institute gate. He wore the familiar dark hat of the villagers, the black suit, shiny with age and possibly dirt, the soiled white collarless shirt; he had the usual thick black moustache and grey hair, the darkly-tanned features. I recognised Ellicott, the original Ellicott, who had scampered before me on all fours on the beach, howling at a non-existent moon.

He gave a start on seeing me, then, without saying a word, turned his back on me and began to walk rapidly down the path. I shouted to him to stop and, when he paid no attention, I ran after him, yelling for him to wait. He glanced over his shoulder and broke into a run. I pursued, determined not to allow him to escape: my sandals pounded slackly on the dust of the road, my breath escaped in harsh gasps. The man was surprisingly nimble; he ran with easy, practised strides, almost effortlessly and keeping a steady distance in front of me. No doubt he would have eluded me completely if, while turning his head to glance triumphantly back at me, he had not struck his foot against a large stone and fallen headlong. Before he could rise, I was on top of him, pinning him to the ground under the full weight of my body.

He struggled futilely for a few moments, then relaxed completely and stared at me impassively. 'I will allow you to get up,' I told him, speaking slowly and distinctly, 'if you promise not to try to escape and to answer all my questions.' He made no reply, but I thought I detected a nod and I raised myself cautiously, alert to pounce once more if he attempted any deceit. He rose to his feet and brushed some dirt from his trousers; his hat had fallen off during our struggle and, instead of replacing it, he held it loosely in his right hand.

'You are Ellicott?' I began.

He glared at me in sullen silence.

'You spoke to me on the beach once, oh, two weeks ago.'

Still no reply.

'You said then that you hated and feared the Institute. What are you doing visiting there?'

I felt like seizing him by the lapels and shaking him out of his surly impassivity, but I controlled myself. 'Have you changed your attitude? Do you no longer fear that your souls will be eaten?'

He sneered. 'Eating souls?' he repeated. 'Why do you talk so crazy?'

'You told me,' I persisted, 'that your souls used to visit the island at night. You said that Dr Daniels had started to interfere with them. So you and some others put up nets to prevent them crossing the sea. You took me down with you to the nets one evening.' I paused, unwilling to push my reminiscences any further unless I had to.

He shrugged his shoulders. 'You think of someone else. There are many Ellicotts here. Many Hansletts. Many Mauretts. There are six, perhaps ten, surnames throughout the village. Find yourself another Ellicott. I have work to do.' He banged his hat violently against his thigh a couple of times, to clean it, and put it back on his head. He nodded brusquely and turned on his heel.

I allowed him to leave, watching his black figure as he bounced, with a peculiarly jaunty stride, over the uneven surface of the road. Perhaps he was telling the truth, though I was still convinced that, if nothing else, he was the man I had spoken to on the beach. I remembered Hanslett's warning that 'Ellicott' was untrustworthy and unreliable, but there seemed nothing I could do to find out who, if anyone, in this area I could believe and rely upon. I set off down the road after him, my feet dragging in the dust, my step not jaunty in the least.

My back, as I had feared it might, began to ache shortly after I reached the hotel. I stripped off my shirt and examined myself in the mirror: the skin over my shoulder blades was already fiery red and I could scarcely bear to touch it. I had brought some lotion with me, in anticipation of such a situation, but found that the skin was too tender for me even to attempt to apply it. I sprinkled it with water as best I could, allowed it to dry, and eased myself into a clean shirt before dinner.

The landlady had prepared one of my favourite meals – cod steaks, fresh from the sea, cooked in the simplest manner possible and garnished only with a squeeze of lemon. I ate with less than my usual appetite, squirming uncomfortably to avoid contact with the back of my chair. She soon became aware that something was wrong and asked, with genuine concern, why I was not enjoying my food. I explained about my back and she offered to take a look at it; gently she pulled the shirt away from my shoulders and uttered a low moan of dismay.

'We must do something about that,' she said.

I told her that I had tried, but could hardly endure even to touch it.

'No, I will help,' she insisted. 'We have herbs here, remedies for everything. Go up to your room and I will join you in a moment.'

I went cautiously upstairs, peeled off my shirt, and lay face down on my bed. She entered almost immediately, carrying a large bottle half full of some murky green liquid. She sat down beside me, murmuring words of consolation, and gently poured some drops of the liquid on my back. Then, with infinite sensitivity, she began to ease them into the skin with her fingertips, moving so lightly that I could feel nothing except a delicious sensation of coolness, blissful relief from the burning and itching of the past hour. I closed my eyes and relaxed. She rubbed with a smooth, circular motion, widening out and then narrowing back towards the centre, repeating the gesture over and over again, and talking to me all the time in a soft, continuous undertone, in which I could make out nothing of the words but from which I derived an immense sense of comfort and well-being. I felt myself drifting off to sleep, her tone was so hypnotic, and I struggled to stay awake, for her actions, though relaxing in one sense, were also extremely erotic and stimulated me to thoughts of renewing my earlier attempts on her. She must have been aware of this for, as I struggled sleepily to reach her with my arm and draw her close to me, she bent her head down to my ear and whispered something that sounded like, 'Wait till tomorrow, we have time enough before us.' I closed my eyes and offered no further resistance.

I could have accounted easily enough for the nightmares that tormented my sleep that night, if my back had not been treated after all and if I had suffered agonies of physical misery and wretchedness, tossing uncomfortably and endlessly on my bed. Instead, I am convinced that I slept soundly, and I know that I awoke with my shoulders completely healed and not the slightest trace of burning or peeling to be seen. Yet my sleep was haunted by hideous and terrifying images that seemed to give me no respite, one series implacably replacing another until everything merged together in a grotesque finale from which I awoke trembling and panting with fear.

Though most of the details had been lost by the time I awoke, and those remaining faded as the day went on, that final segment remained vividly in my mind and proved impossible to shake off. I christened it 'The Burning Rat', after the most horrifying of its many disturbing aspects.

It began in a grotto that I recognised from one of the Seahorse cards. This stretched endlessly around me in all directions and even the roof, from which a series of huge stalactites depended, thick as columns, forming a forest of pillars through which I wandered seeking either an exit or a centre – even the roof was hidden from view. I walked for what seemed like hours, dodging the huge icicles, ducking under some that had grown so closely together that they formed a fence, occasionally even being forced to crawl on my belly to avoid being trapped. No doubt I was proceeding in circles, as if in a maze, and I soon began to recognise definite stages on my journey, identical obstacles that had to be overcome, curious deformations in the ice that had previously caught my attention. For there were stalagmites too, rising many feet from the floor, tapering to points high above my head, and sometimes these had shaped themselves over the centuries into fantastic formations that resembled, though in weird, distorted fashion, animals and birds and plants. As I studied these, they began to change, to melt and grow and reshape themselves, as if the centuries-long process that had created them had suddenly been speeded up before my eyes. They took on a bewildering variety of patterns, some clearly recognisable, others totally meaningless, and a few seeming briefly to have significance, a tangible identity, then losing or altering this just as I was on the point of grasping it. I became aware too of a hollow booming sound, monotonous and inescapable, that accompanied all my wanderings; gradually I realised that this was caused by water dripping from the roofs and walls, and both speeded up and magnified by the freakish conditions that prevailed.

Suddenly, although I knew I was returning to the spot for at least the tenth time, I found that one area had changed: the icicles had retreated to form a watchful circle round an open space, and I recognised the common-room of the boarding-school where I had spent so many years of my childhood. A fire flickered feebly in the open grate; text-books, pens and pencils were scattered over the table; sports equipment and discarded items of clothing had been dumped on the floor. Despite the evidence of daily occupation, I realised that it was the beginning of term and that I was one of the first to arrive.

One of my school-mates had returned before me; he was sitting on the sofa in front of the fire, leaning forward to toast a piece of bread struck on the end of some kind of skewer. I recognised the 'Ellicott' who had taken me out with him in his boat to harvest lobsters: he was dressed as he had been that day, he was the same age, and yet he also belonged in the schoolroom and I greeted him with delighted recognition. We recounted our experiences over the Christmas vacation, we discussed prospects for the coming term, we speculated maliciously as to how our friends and some of the teachers might have amused themselves over the holiday.

I picked up a slice of bread and looked around for a toasting-fork. There was one lying on the far corner of the table and I had to move round the sofa to reach it. My foot landed on something soft and yielding that squealed with pain and terror; I looked down in surprise and saw a young rat staring up at me with piteous, pleading eyes. 'Don't hurt me,' it begged. 'I don't want you to hurt me.'

I withdrew my foot and continued to gaze at the creature. 'What is it?' Ellicott demanded

'A rat,' I muttered, not looking at him.

'The place is infested with them,' he complained bitterly. 'They've been crawling all over me ever since I got back. Hand it over here, I'll deal with it.'

I stooped to pick the creature up, but it squirmed away from me, wriggling on its side and flailing its paws helplessly. 'Please don't,' it pleaded. 'Please don't hurt me.' It opened its mouth and began to scream, a high-pitched, monotonous wail, like a hungry, desperate child.

I hesitated once more. 'What's the matter?' Ellicott insisted impatiently. 'Hand it over here and let me deal with it.'

I looked around for something by which to lift the rodent, for I shrank now from actually touching it. I reached over for the toasting-fork and scooped the rat on to it, prodding it with my foot, and trying to ignore the whimpers that had replaced the screaming. I offered the fork to Ellicott, who picked the beast up by its tail and held it close before his eyes, dangling it gently back and forth.

'Pooh!' he grunted disgustedly and, with a casual flick of his wrist, he tossed the rat on to the fire.

I expected it to resist, to attempt to scramble out, and I held the fork ready to poke it back into the flames. I had not wanted this to happen, but now that it was under way, it seemed more merciful in the long run to co-operate with Ellicott and get it all over quickly. But the creature made no move to escape; it sat there with the flames lapping round it, gazing at me with mournful, soulful reproach. For the longest time the fire seemed to have no effect on it, not even singeing its skin; I wondered whether it might not be possible after all to rescue it, to pluck it out with the tongs that leant against the side of the fireplace. But even as I thought this, it began to crumble, to disintegrate, dissolving quietly into a heap of dust and ashes; before it did so, however, it made one last statement: 'Granted!' it squeaked, fixing me implacably with its eyes, 'Granted!' Then there was silence, the coals collapsed over the sudden void, a brief spurt of flame flared up that lingered in the updraught, was caught up into smoke and whirled away.

On my way to the Institute in the morning, I pondered the meaning of the rat's final cry of 'Granted!' Was this simply the recognition and acceptance of an adversary's superior strength, a realisation that its fate was sealed and further resistance was useless? Or had it a more metaphysical significance, had the creature – as I remembered suspecting at the time – reached to some hidden level within me and extracted some secret that, once confronted or acknowledged, might change the whole direction of my life, a secret whose meaning, summed up in the code word, 'Granted!', had been obvious enough in my dream but, now that I was awake, required to be laboriously deciphered or unlocked once again?

I shook my head, impatient with my fancies. A dream was only a dream, there was meaning in it, no doubt, but not of the kind for which I was searching. I knew it was a common enough experience for someone to awaken from a dream certain that he had solved the riddle of existence, to scrawl this down on a sheet of paper, and discover in the morning that he had written nothing but mere gibberish. The dream disturbed me nevertheless; I had not been conscious of dreaming since I arrived in the village – though no doubt I had done so, often enough – and I wondered what had caused me to experience something so elaborate and so vivid.

I heard the clatter of hooves behind me and the rattle of wheels. I stepped aside automatically, without looking back, and a donkey slowly drew level with me, drawing a small cart. It was driven by an old man, his face grizzled and lined; he nodded briefly as he passed me, keeping his eyes fixed on the road ahead. His wife sat inside the cart, clutching on her knee a large bundle wrapped up in a cloth. She wore the shapeless black clothing of the village women and a shawl over her head concealed her features almost completely from view; only the tip of her nose peered out, and a twist of grey hair. On this section of the path, their destination could only be the Institute, and I wondered idly what business they had there – delivering clean laundry, perhaps.

Maria, as before, greeted me when I arrived at the gate. 'You don't really need to announce your arrival, you

know,' she told me. 'You can just start work right away.'
I explained, half-jokingly, that I wanted her to know that
I was carrying out my obligations, though, in reality, I
continued to hope that I might be invited to enter the
Institute and have the opportunity to meet Dr Daniels
and the mysterious second woman. She said she would
bring me lunch again at noon, and drifted off into the
building again.

The wind was much colder on the cliff top that morning,
and I wished that I had thought to bring a sweater with
me. I worked with much less enthusiasm than before,
often breaking off to huddle in the shelter of the wall to
escape from the cold; but my main problem was that, the
more I considered it, the less satisfactory my earlier work
appeared to be. Yesterday everything had been easy, almost automatic: I had felt that, whatever it was I was
shaping, it had its own interior logic, a secret design that
would reveal itself when the time was ripe, perhaps only
at the very last moment, the instant of completion. Now,
however, it seemed nothing but a shapeless and meaningless mess, a ramshackle conglomeration of random
elements, clues that led nowhere, harmonies that, even as
I contemplate them, dissolved and collapsed into raucous
discordance.

Gradually I found that, instead of adding to my construction, I was, almost unconsciously, beginning to strip
away and discard segments – a leaf here, a pebble there
to begin with, and then larger and more complex elements,
until I was attacking the very substance of the construction itself, the framework that had given it whatever
significance it had once possessed. I found that I took
almost as much joy in the process of dismantling as I had
previously done in that of creation; I began to work with
total absorption at ripping the statue apart and reducing

it once more to its component elements. Despite the cold, I found that I was sweating vigorously, my shirt clung damply to my body and my hair slicked forward into my eyes, though I was too preoccupied even to push it away. Not content with merely scattering rocks and branches around me, I began to heave some of them over the edge of the cliff into the sea, and I welcomed the faint splashes that followed with a grim smile.

At exactly the moment that I had reduced the statue to a pile of rubble once more, Maria appeared round the corner of the wall carrying a tray of food. She stopped short, staring with amazement at the devastation I had carried out, but, instead of protesting, she merely shrugged and continued her advance. 'Not having too good a morning?' she murmured sympathetically as she set the tray down on the grass and squatted beside it.

'On the contrary,' I replied, 'I've never felt more creative in my life.'

I sat down beside her. The wind riffled through her shoulder-length black hair, driving it now away from her face, now back in front of her eyes and cheeks, so that she brushed it aside impatiently with her hand. I picked up a slice of bread and smeared it with pâté. I took a large bite and, deliberately speaking with my mouth full, I told her that I didn't think I would be doing any more sculpting for the time being. She had difficulty in understanding me and, when I repeated myself, I found that I had made the phrasing more courteous, less bluntly hostile. 'I don't see any point in starting again,' I told her. 'Whatever gifts I may have, they are not in this direction.'

I shivered in the wind and coughed unexpectedly. I was concerned that I might catch a chill from my damp shirt and so welcomed her suggestion that we move into the lee of the wall for shelter. I wanted to take the chance to suggest that we actually enter the building, but realised that my failures of the morning could hardly entitle me to any special concessions.

'I don't mean to be unhelpful,' I went on, after we had moved. 'It's just that I don't really see the point of all this in any case. You say you want to leave something behind for the villagers when you go, to thank them for helping you. Well, I haven't seen much evidence of co-operation from them so far, for a start, and from what I can see, most of them seem to hate you and fear you. And if you *have* had help, why not reward them in a more tangible and practical way? – they could certainly do with it. You must be aware of the poverty here, the lack of most decent amenities.'

'They seem happy enough, though,' she murmured.

'That's easy for you to say. You come here and live in privileged conditions for a few weeks, you can leave whenever you want to. They have to stay here, whether you think they're happy or not.'

'Maybe they have a secret we've lost. Maybe they don't need material goods and comforts the way we do.'

I thought of the useless television sets and refrigerators, the dishwashers and the computers, and I felt disappointed in her. I had expected something better of Maria than this fake-liberal sentimentality about primitive squalor, the wide-eyed and yet wilfully blind romanticising of living conditions that she herself would not tolerate for a week. I decided to change the subject.

'Do you know anything about a large grotto near here?' I enquired. 'Either on the mainland, or perhaps on the island?'

She gave a start and examined me with renewed interest. 'Maybe,' she ventured cautiously. 'Tell me more about it.'

I said that I had first seen it on one of the Seahorse cards and then had dreamt about it the previous evening. I described it as best I could, paying particular attention to the weird shapes and grotesque animal-like formations I had discovered inside it. She listened with rapt eagerness, her lips slightly parted, nodding quickly whenever I paused and urging me to go on. When I had finished, she leaned back against the wall and exhaled a long, slow sigh.

'Yes, there is a grotto like that – *exactly* like that – on the island. But hardly anyone is allowed to visit it. The island is – taboo is the wrong word – sacred for the villagers. It's where they believe their souls travel in the evenings, when their bodies are asleep. They sport and frolic on the sands.'

I was struck by her use of the word 'frolic' to describe the souls' activities, but was more concerned with testing to what extent she was telling me the full truth. 'You say very few people see the grotto,' I probed. 'Have you been there yourself?'

'No,' she replied glibly and, I thought, rather too quickly. 'We're not allowed even to set foot on the island. But Ellicott and some others have described the grotto to us very minutely, and it's just as you say it is. This is very curious.'

What was even more curious, I mused, somewhat ungraciously, was that she should persist in lying to me so blatantly and attempting to deceive me about her group's nocturnal visits to the island. Though it was just possible, I conceded, that they never actually landed on the island and merely circled it and observed it for their own mysterious purposes.

'They have ceremonies on the island, though,' she continued, as though aware of my mistrust, 'and outsiders can watch these from a distance, from boats on the open sea. There is one of these due in a couple of days, in fact, at full moon. We saw the preparations for it in the square a few days ago. The Walking on Water.'

She seemed on the point of explaining more about this, when we were interrupted by a young woman who turned the corner of the wall, walking quite quickly, and almost stumbled over us. She recovered her poise immediately and stood, with legs spread slightly apart and hands on hips, staring down at us.

'So this is where you are,' she said to Maria. Her gaze passed on to me. 'And this must be the friend you told me about, your Mr Overage.'

I protested, as usual in vain, that that was not the way to pronounce it. Without making any physical gesture, she gave the impression of sweeping my remonstrances into insignificance, and my voice trailed away into silence. She was quite stunningly beautiful, tall and slim, with hair so dark that, as she tossed it back now and then to counteract the displacements of the wind, it took on an almost bluish sheen. She wore a pair of tight jeans that hugged close to every outline of her hips and legs, and a faded brown man's shirt, casually unbuttoned to reveal small, but firm and shapely breasts.

She looked away from us towards where the statue had stood. 'Not making much progress, are you?' she reflected.

Maria rose to her feet and I struggled up beside her. 'This is Martina,' she told me. 'David's fiancée.' She spoke with a trace of hostility, even perhaps jealousy, and I gazed at the newcomer open-mouthed, trying to assimilate this new information. I would never have associated Davers with someone as elegant and sophisticated as this; I had automatically placed her in the category of women denied to me for all purposes except casual friendship and frustrated admiration from afar, and Davers seemed, if anything, even less suited to her than I would be.

I realised that she was contemplating me with an amused smile, and I hastily switched my gaze away from her. 'The statue,' I mumbled, 'well, I had some problems with it this morning. Need to rethink it. Start again tomorrow.' I fell silent again and stared at the ground in front of my toes, where a caterpillar was easing its way across the grass, hump and flatten, hump and flatten.

'I'm sure you'll make a wonderful job of it.' Her voice was clear and musical, yet still with a tinge of amusement to it. 'I know we're all relying on you to produce something quite sensational.'

I felt that she was making fun of me and, though Maria had done this too, there had been a sense of cameraderie, even, I imagined, affection, in her treatment of me. This newcomer, on the other hand, was distant, superior, perhaps contemptuous, and I felt uncomfortable about submitting myself to her taunts any longer.

'I'll be going now,' I said to Maria. 'I'll come back tomorrow morning and try again. But don't expect too much of me. Thanks for the lunch.' I nodded briefly to Martina and turned away from them. I imagined whispers, sniggers, stifled laughter as I walked away, though all I actually heard was the inevitable cicadas, the screams of gulls wheeling in the cloudy sky.

There was little that I could do for the remainder of the afternoon and neither the landlord nor his wife was to be seen when I arrived back at the hotel. I stretched myself out on my bed, with my hands folded under my head, and, in the half-dozing condition that followed, I began to wonder if I had interpreted the landlady correctly when she had seemed to suggest a rendezvous today. I was not even sure that I wished to become involved with her at all, but I still felt resentful of Martina's disparaging treatment of me and needed to prove, if only to myself, that not all women would reject and scorn me.

I swung my feet off the bed and paused, sitting there, listening for any sounds from within the hotel or in the street. It must still be the siesta time, I thought, for everything was totally quiet, except for a curious grinding sound that seemed to come from a lower floor of the hotel. I pushed my feet into my sandals and moved cautiously out into the corridor. The sound was louder now, and definitely came from the direction of the kitchen; I made my way downstairs and padded softly towards the door. Keeping myself concealed behind the frame, I peered warily into the room. The landlady was standing with her back to me, stooped over, and totally absorbed in some task; shifting my position slightly, I saw that she was sharpening a carving knife on a grindstone, whetting its edge with scrupulous and expert attention. An assortment of knives lay beside her on the counter, in an astonishing range of shapes and sizes – far larger than I would have imagined necessary for the limited type of cooking she was required to perform. All these must have been sharpened already, and the late afternoon sunlight that slanted in through the window glinted wickedly on the blades.

From the room immediately to my left came a sudden groan, a moan of fear and pure terror, a gibbering of incomprehensible words in a tone of abject entreaty. The landlady stopped work, cocked her head to listen, then, calmly and methodically, she gathered up the knives and put them away in a drawer. She smoothed her hands down on her apron and turned towards the door.

I ducked back into the dining-room and sat down at

one of the tables. The landlady came through the doorway and, at the same moment, the door to what must be their bedroom opened and the landlord stepped out. He was even more rumpled and dishevelled than usual, his loose shirt flapped open to reveal his hairy paunch, and his stained, ill-fitting trousers drooped below his belly, the fly unbuttoned. He was unshaven and bleary-eyed and he moved his hand vaguely over the stubble as if that would somehow remove it and make him reasonably presentable once more. He narrowed his eyes suspiciously when he saw me and glanced from me to his wife and back again. I noticed that she gave a small, almost imperceptible shake of the head and smiled faintly. He lumbered towards me and thumped a hairy hand, with its long and rarely-cleaned fingernails, on the table. He brought his face to within a foot of mine and stared at me in silence.

I stammered that I had thought – being, as he knew, without a watch – that it might be time for the evening meal – no doubt I was early and I would be happy to leave until the correct time arrived.

He shook his head. 'No,' he said, 'this time you come with me and you really learn Seahorse. We have two hours till eating.' He straightened up and grasped my arm firmly, forcing me to stand up too. He led me towards the door. I managed to swivel round and stare pleadingly at the landlady before we went out, but she merely stood with arms folded, leaning against the doorframe, still with that faint smile on her lips.

The landlord marched me down the street, despite my assurances that, if he would only let go of me and allow me to walk freely, I would accompany him without protest. The sun was lower in the sky now and the shadows lengthened around us. The usual group of

Seahorse players were already gathered in the tavern, absorbed in a game. The landlord found a spare chair, brought it to the table, and thrust me into it. He stood beside me, whispering instructions into my ear, but mumbling so rapidly and fracturing his pidgin English so much more incoherently even than usual, that I remained totally at a loss as to how I should proceed.

I was dealt some cards and a pile of counters was placed before me. With a practised gesture of his right hand, the landlord swept them out in a long line before me on the table and quickly rearranged the colours, that to me were almost indistinguishable, into a recognisable pattern that began with bright blue on the left and gradually changed, through almost imperceptible gradations, to darker shades of blue, a mixture of blue and green, and finally a sombre and murky type of true green. He then gathered these together in half a dozen piles and nodded cordially for me to begin.

I studied the cards in my hand. *Grotto* and *Martyr* I was familiar with; then came, as always when I was forced to undergo this ordeal, a new card that bewildered and frightened me, riveting my attention and making it impossible for me to offer any participation in the game around me. This time the photograph was of a rat, squatting on its haunches in a fireplace, totally encircled by flames and peering calmly over them, its nose wrinkled, its features alert. The landlord bent close to me to examine it, his stale breath warm on my cheek, and clicked his tongue in disapproval. '*Burning Rat* is bad luck,' he muttered.

I pulled myself together, for this time I was determined not to allow whatever trickery they might be performing to have the desired effect on me. It was clear enough, in any case, what was involved in this instance: I must have noticed the card before, when I had last participated in a game, probably while I was searching the pack for the missing *Wolf Hunt*. It had not registered on me consciously at the time, but must have returned when I was asleep – just as the *Grotto* card had also insinuated itself into my thoughts – and had taken its place in the dream-narrative, perhaps even helping to shape and determine it.

The complacency with which I accepted this solution was utterly destroyed by the next card, which once again I recognised from the last game, though it was only now that its significance became evident to me. The object tumbling down the side of the cliff was Davers' statue; the astonished face peering over the edge was my own. If the photograph had been taken from the boat, it would have required a searchlight to illuminate the scene adequately; more to the point, however, how could the photo have been taken before the event occurred?

'Play that one!' the landlord howled unexpectedly in my ear. He plucked the card from my hand and hurled it triumphantly on to the table. A glittering cascade of counters followed, more cards were pushed into my hand. I sat as if in a daze, allowing the landlord to do as he wanted with the cards I held. My head spun with the noise around me, the shouts, the yells, the curses, the arguments, the air was sultry and oppressive. I tried to loosen my shirt but found the collar was unbuttoned already. I surveyed the activities around me in total incomprehension, grinning benignly and nodding inanely whenever someone caught my eye. Finally someone thrust a glass of wine into my hand, I was told that I had won the game, that no one had seen play as skilful as that in the village for years. I was thumped on the back in congratulation, the wine jerked out of the glass and spilled over my shirt, the glass was refilled, I drank it down, I was offered another and another, at last the landlord and some others led me home, half-carrying me. I was taken up to bed, the men withdrew, the landlady entered, expertly she undressed me, she undressed herself, she lay down beside me, she nuzzled my ear with her sharp, pointed teeth, she bit my earlobe, tenderly. I turned my head to look out of the window, the moon was full, all but a slight fragment, the merest nibble, it was set exactly in the centre of the window pane, the four frames touched it, top and bottom, left and right, I had never seen a moon so bright, so dazzling. I closed my eyes, what is your name, I asked her, Ella, she said, Ella Ellicott, we all have such names, Hannah Hanslett is another and Maureen Maurett, they come down to us through the centuries, you knew that, didn't you?, yes, I answered, or no, I don't remember, and I slept.

I gave that night's dream the title, 'Trying to Kill Amin', after the personality that dominated it. I was in a large, whitewashed room, lying on a divan. There were two large windows in the wall directly opposite me and through them I could see nothing but reddish sand, stretching flat and featureless until, about a third of the way up the window, it was cut off, in a rigidly straight line, by the intense radiance of the sky. A man was sitting at a desk positioned exactly between the two windows, writing, with his back turned to me. He was dressed in army uniform and, though I could see little except the thick folds of black skin that creased his neck, I knew instantly who he was. Above my head a fan turned, slackly, endlessly, barely stirring the air and creating the only sound in the room.

I held my breath, waiting for something to happen. A

man entered through the open door, a white man, dressed in a soiled and crumpled white suit. He glanced at me, put his finger to his lips and winked at me, slowly, grotesquely, confidentially. Without waiting for my response, he began to move cautiously across the room, walking on tiptoes on the points of running-shoes that had once been white but were now streaked with dirt. One of the shoes was unlaced: the metal tips of the laces dragged behind him, scraping almost imperceptibly on the concrete floor, but the man at the desk seemed not to hear.

The newcomer took up position directly behind Amin. I realised that he was holding a green wine bottle in his hand, still full and corked, with a label that I was unable to decipher. Slowly he raised the bottle above his head, to the full extent of his right arm and, after what seemed an endless pause, he brought it down savagely on the head of the man before him. The bottle smashed to pieces, red liquid poured down the back of the man's head, over his uniform, over the back of the chair. He made no movement, no sound, he merely continued writing. The man in white stood as if transfixed, his hand dangling by his side and still holding the neck of the broken bottle, with its jagged shards of glass; finally he turned to face me. He gave an almost comical shrug and spread his arms wide as if to ask what more he could do; he tossed the remnants of the bottle into a corner, shattering it still further, and, without any attempt at concealment, walked briskly out of the room, the soles of his shoes slapping loudly against the floor. Amin continued writing, and gave no sign of having noticed him.

There was another long pause. The light outside the window began to fade and, with tropical swiftness, the night arrived. The full moon became visible in the bottom left-hand corner of one of the windows; it swung rapidly upwards until it was framed exactly in the centre of the window, touching it on all sides. It hung there, dazzling and immobile. I realised that another man had entered the room and was already half-way towards the desk. This time he was black, he crept noiselessly forward on bare feet, and he carried a large carving knife in his right hand. He too stationed himself immediately behind Amin, holding the knife loosely by his side.

With unbelievable rapidity, and so quickly that the first blow had been struck before I had even realised what was happening, the man stabbed Amin in the back, just below the neck and towards the right shoulder. He pulled the knife free and struck again. With each blow he raised the weapon high above his head, so that it glinted briefly in the moonlight. With each blow he grunted, and muttered something in a language I could not understand.

I expected Amin to slump forward over his desk, arms sprawling, sending documents and paper fluttering to the floor; but once again he paid no attention to what was happening. Blood poured from the wounds in his back, occasionally his shoulders twitched as if he were shrugging something away, but he made no sound. Finally his attacker paused, baffled, gazing in disgust at the useless weapon in his hand.

Now, at last, Amin stood up, scraping his chair back along the floor with a harsh, grating sound that reverberated suddenly in the silent room. He turned to face his adversary, who stood staring at him, paralysed with terror. Amin beamed, a huge smile split his face from ear to ear, his teeth gleamed with dazzling whiteness in his dark face. He stepped closer and put his arms round the man's waist, hugging him tightly to him. The knife clattered to the floor and spun wildly for a few moments, until it came to rest with the blade pointing directly at me.

Amin held the man fast in a grip from which it would be impossible to escape, though he in fact put up no resistance and seemed resigned to his fate. I could see Amin's face over the other's shoulder, the teeth clenched now, the brow furrowed with exertion, beads of sweat standing on his forehead. He gave a grunt and then, with an appalling crack, the man's ribs snapped. The victim made no sound, not even a whimper of pain, but his body slumped slackly in Amin's arms and his head lolled on his shoulder. Amin held him for some time longer, squeezing him gently in a grotesque parody of an affectionate embrace; his eye caught mine as I stared at him open-mouthed and he closed it in a long, slow wink that suggested complicity, understanding. He let the body fall to the floor and stood over it, feet set firmly apart, his hands planted on his hips. He looked up at me and smiled.

I awoke with my throat dry and seemingly coated with a thick fuzz like the surface of a thousand caterpillars. My head was remarkably clear, though I could remember few details of the previous evening. I recalled the landlady's visit, but there were no signs of her presence in the bed beside me, no indentation in pillow or sheet to reveal that another body had rested there.

Cautiously, I stood up and walked over to the bathroom. I took a drink of the tepid and no doubt insanitary water that trickled from the tap, and splashed my face to clear it of the sweat and grime that had collected the previous evening. As I straightened up, my elbow jogged a tiny mirror that someone had recently hung on a nail to the left of the wash-basin; the touch dislodged it and, before I could do anything to catch it, it had fallen and shattered on the floor. I wondered who could have put it there – the landlady, no doubt, for she seemed not to share her husband's concern about avoiding reflections.

I gathered up the pieces and looked round for somewhere to deposit them. There was no waste-basket, of course, and I finally had to leave them in a pile by the door in the hope that, whenever the room was next cleaned, they would be removed. The mirror on the dressing-table was covered with the usual black cloth; I stretched out my hand to remove this, then hesitated and decided not to. I had an odd feeling that I wouldn't very much like whatever I might see if I took down the cloth, and that it might be wiser to forbear.

There was no one to be seen in the kitchen or the dining-room and, as I often did, I helped myself to a breakfast of bread and a glass of milk. It must have rained overnight, for the sultriness of the previous evening had gone and the heat had not yet built up to the almost intolerable level of some of the preceding days. I decided to take a swim before I went up to the Institute, hoping to freshen myself up that way and make myself rather more presentable than I felt at the moment.

I met no one whom I recognised as I went down to the sea and the beach itself was virtually deserted. A man had caught a squid and was methodically beating it to death against a large rock; when he was satisfied that the job was finished, he banged it twice against his right thigh as a concluding gesture and set off back for the village. He nodded cordially as he passed me.

I stripped down to my bathing suit and took a vigorous run into the water. It was unexpectedly cold at first, but a few minutes' splashing and ducking myself under the surface warmed me up. I swam about a hundred yards out from the shore, where the water was still shallow and I remained comfortably within my depth, and rolled over to float on my back. I squinted up at the sun through half-closed eyes and lay with the water rocking me gently, lapping my ears now with a hollow, booming sound and now with a soft bubbling. The current swung me round till my feet were pointing towards the Institute; if I raised my head slightly, I could see the building itself and the headland where my statue was supposed to stand.

There was a sudden splashing in the water beside me and a hand touched my shoulder, tipping me slightly so that I lost my equilibrium and flailed around for a moment or two, driving water into my mouth and eyes, before I could recover my balance. My feet found the bottom at last and I glared round indignantly to see who had disturbed me.

The other woman from the Institute, Martina, was standing about a yard away, smiling at me with what seemed faint mockery. The water reached to just below her breasts, which were bare and deeply tanned from the sun. I gaped at her and then averted my eyes.

'We've met before,' she said, with ludicrous formality, stretching her hand towards me. 'I'm Martina Massingham.'

I clasped her hand briefly but said nothing, suspecting that, if I repeated my name, she would deliberately mangle it once more.

'Isn't it lovely here?' she went on amicably, stooping to splash some water on her breasts. 'It's just perfect for swimming.'

I said that I was just about to leave, as I had my work to do at the Institute.

'Oh, don't bother about that.' She stretched out her arm, as if to detain me. 'It's not worth it any longer.

We're leaving tomorrow. Or the next day. At any rate, after the Walking on Water.'

I asked when that took place.

'Tonight or tomorrow. It has to be at full moon, but also it has to be completely cloudless. Otherwise, so they say, it won't work and the children will sink.'

I remembered the scenes at the fountain a few days ago. 'You don't mean that they expect children actually to walk on the water?' I asked incredulously. 'But that's impossible.'

She shrugged. 'That's what they say. They do it in relays. From about half a mile out from shore, to the island, depending on how many children have qualified each year. Each one does about a hundred yards. They have boats to protect them if anything goes wrong.' She shivered. 'I'm getting cold. I'll race you out to that rock and back again.'

She was a powerful swimmer and had completed her circuit while I was still struggling round the half-way marker. She swam part of the way back to meet me and circled me playfully once or twice, like a dolphin accompanying some shipwrecked sailor. We came out of the water side by side and she stretched herself flat on her back on the sand, shielding her eyes from the sun. I sat beside her with my knees drawn up to my middle and my hands clasping them.

On the rock at the entrance to the bay, the woman I had noticed once before was sitting, her golden hair gleaming in the sunlight. A faint noise, as of song, came towards us over the water. 'Who is that?' I asked Martina. 'She can't be from the village, her hair's the wrong colour. But I thought there were only you and Maria at the Institute.'

'It must be the mermaid,' she answered casually, without even looking up. 'She's usually out there at this time.'

I uttered something between a snort and a laugh, uncertain how seriously to take this. 'You're joking,' I suggested finally.

'There's quite a colony of them out there.' Her voice was unemphatic, even indifferent, as if it scarcely mattered whether I believed her or not. 'There are the usual legends in the village about inter-marriage, desertion, betrayal, tragic love affairs, blandishments, seductions, jealousies, murders. You're a writer, aren't you?' She rolled over on to her stomach and surveyed me thoughtfully. 'That's what Maria tells me anyway. I'd have thought this would be an ideal subject for you. You should borrow a boat one morning and go out and visit her. But don't get too close and be careful to stop up your ears to protect yourself from her siren song. Unless you want to stay here for ever, that is, under her spell.' Though she affected a tone of almost childish, awestruck exaggeration in these last words, this was strangly belied by the serious, level gaze of her grey eyes. Once again I was uncertain how to respond.

'You say you're all leaving here soon,' I offered. 'You must have finished all your researches then?'

She nodded and said nothing.

'Curious place, this,' I went on. 'Quite a treasure trove for researchers in every field, I should think. As for me, I'm just an amateur, I'll write about anything that pays. A bit of this, a bit of that. Travel around. It's easy enough when you haven't any family, any ties.'

Martina was scooping a hole in the sand and then allowing the grains to trickle back through her fingers into their original position. It was clear that either she was not listening to me or, if she was, she did not believe me.' I hear you're engaged to Davers,' I said abruptly.

'Who?' she asked vaguely, staring up at me. 'Oh, you mean David. Yes, I suppose we are, in a way.'

'I'm sure I've heard of him. He's written a book, hasn't he?'

'David?' The sand worked its way back through her fingers, and now she was creating a series of little mounds all round the edge of the pit she had excavated. 'No, nothing like that. He's the only one of us, though, who's actually been in the Tower.'

'The Tower?'

'Over there.' Without looking she gestured randomly behind her to where the island brooded, low and squat, on the water, the broken finger of the tower the only relief in its flat monotony.

'So he's actually been there? Set foot on it?'

'Yes. But don't tell anyone in the village. We're not supposed to go out there.'

Then why was she confiding in *me*, a complete outsider, I wondered, about whom she knew nothing? 'What is so special about the tower?' I asked.

'It's something to do with the statue, you know, on the fountain. The man who designed it, centuries ago, lived out there in the tower, a recluse.'

'The Saint Sebastian?'

'What? Oh, you've been listening to David. He has no more idea of what it is than I have. That's just his theory, that's all.'

'Why don't you ask the villagers?'

'They don't know either. And anyway, you can't trust them. They'll tell you anything you want to hear.' She raised her hand higher, allowed the sand to drizzle through the very tips of her fingers. The wind caught it and floated it away. 'I think it's a sex scene of some kind, an orgy. It was destroyed, you know, immediately after it was completed. The outraged citizens marched together in a body to pull it down, that kind of thing. David says it was because the figure of the Saint was too brutal, too graphic in its pain. *I* think they thought it was too dirty.' She chuckled. 'They made a half-hearted attempt to build it up again later, but they lost interest before it was completed. David thinks that part of the problem might be that the second design was a totally different concept from the first and the two are inextricably confused.'

'What about the designer?'

'Oh, he hanged himself, I think. Or cut his throat. In the tower. They were setting out in boats to lynch him, in any case. Or so the story goes.'

'Was he called Ellicott?'

She rolled over on her back again, propping herself up on her elbows. Her breasts jutted upwards, the nipples firm and pointed. 'Yes. How did you know?'

'Just a guess. It was either that, or Hanslett.'

'Or Maurett. And there are a few people called Lincott, though they're very low in the village hierarchy. It took the Ellicotts centuries to live down their disgrace, though they've got over it now.'

I realised with a start that the tide had crept up on us during our conversation and was lapping around our toes. 'What time is it?' I asked her.

'I don't know. Around lunch-time, I suppose.' She stood up and brushed the sand from her trim buttocks. 'I'll go and put my clothes on.' She had left them in a neat pile a few yards higher up the beach; before leaving, she began to kick down the mounds of sand she had created as we talked. I tried to stop her for, towards the end, she had been working with wet sand from the bottom of the pool she had dredged and, out of this, she had created a small but elaborate sculpture, fantastically twisted and adorned, that suddenly reminded me of one of the stalagmites I had seen in my dream of the grotto. Before I could confirm this, however, the object was in ruins.

I caught up with her as she was buttoning up her blouse. She tossed her head back and shook her hair to free it of any sand that had caught there. 'I'll have to go back to the hotel and change,' I explained, 'but would you like to join me for lunch?

She smiled and shook her head. 'No, the others will expect me back. But you can buy me a drink if you like.'

I pulled my shirt and trousers over my uncomfortably wet bathing suit and we walked in silence up the steps. Martina suggested that we pass first through the square, so that she could explain to me her theory about the statue. We studied the worn and battered stones carefully. 'Look,' she indicated with a finger, circling a rough outline in the air, 'there are at least three or four bodies there, one of them probably an animal. That would make it a really interesting orgy. And they're obviously grappling together, intertwined. Just use your imagination a little, or perhaps you don't need to imagine it, just remember instead.' She fixed me with her clear grey eyes, her lips curled in a faint smile.

'What do you mean?' I protested. 'I've never been involved in anything like that.'

'Haven't you? But surely you can see what I mean all the same?'

I made a pretence of agreeing with her interpretation, though in reality it seemed even less plausible to me than either of the others. We set off towards the tavern, passing the hotel on the way, where the landlord lounged messily against the door frame, still unshaven and with an unusual airof lassitude about him, as though he had slept badly the previous night. He nodded uneasily as we passed and surveyed Martina with a stare that was partly predatory and appraising, and partly openly hostile.

The tavern was virtually empty, with only a couple of drinkers, survivors perhaps from the previous evening, slumped at a table in the far corner. We were served by a young girl, perhaps sixteen years old, who was dressed in a drab and ill-fitting black dress with a high neck and long sleeves. She had thick lips and sallow cheeks and gazed at us dully from her black eyes, yet it occurred to me that, with a little assistance, she could be made to look reasonably attractive. Though I had heard a good deal of noise from children since my arrival, I had actually *seen* very few, apart from those who had been undergoing the ordeal, or test, at the fountain. I had assumed that they were at school during the day – though I had not come across any building that might serve for that purpose – and in bed after dark. All those that I had seen, however, whatever their age, were dressed like miniature adults, in black dresses and shawls, or in absurdly scaled-down black suits and hats. I tried to ask the girl where everyone had gone to, but she merely shook her head as if she did not understand the question.

We drank in silence for some time, staring out at the empty, sun-drenched street. I wanted to ask Martina more about her companions and about the Institute itself, but suspected that a direct question would be met with evasiveness or mockery. 'Where do you go after this?' I ventured finally.

She gestured vaguely with her right hand. 'Back home.'

'Which is where?'

'I expect we'll do some travelling first though.' She seemed to feel that this had answered my question, for she looked around her once more and began to tap impatiently on the table with her long finger-nails. 'God, it's so dull here!' she exclaimed suddenly. 'I don't know how you can stand it.' She rose abruptly from the table, scraping her chair back with a harsh, grating sound that reverberated suddenly in the quiet room, and walked over to a nearby table where someone had left a pack of Seahorse cards. She brought them back to our table and began to flick through them idly.

'Have you ever played this?' she asked me.

'I've tried to, or been forced to. But I can't get the hang of it.'

'I'm not surprised. The rules keep changing all the time.' She gave a chuckle on seeing one of the cards and passed it over to me. 'Have you come across this one yet?'

The card showed myself, glaring straight ahead, my mouth half-open, a lock of hair flopping over my forehead. The photo – for, as usual, it could be nothing else – must have been taken after the game of Seahorse in which I discovered that the *Wolf Hunt* card no longer existed and *Martyr* had taken its place. I remembered adopting exactly that ridiculous posture, mouthing those ineffectual and disregarded protests. 'How do they do it?' I asked her, handing the card back and affecting a merely casual interest in the whole business.

'Do what?'

'Those photographs. Or whatever they are.'

'You'll have to ask David, that's his concern. Or Damon.'

'Damon?'

'Dr Daniels.'

'And how do I get to talk to them?'

She made no answer, for her attention was fixed on another of the cards that she had turned over. She let out an unexpected yelp of laughter and jerked back in her chair, tilting it to such an alarming angle that I expected it to tip right over. She straightened up again, her whole body still heaving with unexplained mirth, and clutching the card so tightly in her hand that I was unable to make out what had caused all this.

I gave her time to calm down and asked what the joke was. She shook her head soundlessly, her eyes swimming with tears.

'Let me see the card then.' I stretched out my hand, but she merely huddled her whole body together, with both hands clasping the card to her breast.

'Let me see it.' I was becoming impatient, even angry, with her secretiveness. I stood up and came round to her side of the table. 'Let me see it.'

She shook her head. I attempted to seize the card, grasping her wrist with one hand and beginning to prise open her fingers with the other. The struggle brought me very close to her, my cheek almost touching hers, my hands brushing against her breast as we wrestled for possession. Suddenly she opened her hands wide and allowed the card to flutter on to her lap; I found that I was exerting pressure where there was no longer any resistance and, in an attempt to avoid overbalancing, I steadied myself by placing my hand on her shoulder. I stood there for a moment, gazing at the card, which had fallen face downward; I was distractingly aware of her body close to me and found that I could see most of the way down her blouse to her gently heaving breasts – though there was no logical reason why these should prove more exciting in their present half-concealed, mildly agitated condition, than when they had been openly displayed a foot away from me on the beach.

She made no attempt to pick up the card, which was

balanced precariously at the point where her tight jeans covered her crotch. As I stretched my hand tentatively towards it, she slapped me playfully on the wrist: 'Naughty,' she breathed, smiling at me mischievously. 'Doesn't belong to you. Don't poach.'

Flushing, I snatched it up and withdrew to my own side of the table. I turned the card over and discovered the picture I had seen before of the man and woman copulating like animals – only now both had their faces towards the camera and could be clearly identified. One, as I had suspected, was the landlady; the other, blatantly penetrating her from behind, clasping her breasts one in each hand, his mouth open, the tongue lolling out as if in exquisite parody of his animal-like posture – this other was myself.

I stared at the photograph in horror, trying to organise my thoughts. If it was genuine, it must have been taken the previous evening, at a stage when I had lost all awareness of my surroundings and of what was happening to me. I examined it again, trying vainly to focus on the image that swirled and shifted before my eyes: there was no clue as to whether it had been taken indoors or outside, the figures were seen as if in a void, sharply outlined against a totally black background.

My face was crimson with shame; I felt that I could not walk the streets of the village again, enter the tavern, look any of the inhabitants in the eye. Before I could tear the card up, Martina, who must have sensed my intention, had plucked it out of my hands. 'It's no use,' she murmured softly, and with unexpected sympathy. 'They can make as many more as they like. Some of them much worse than this. What are you worried about anyway? So there's a picture of you humping the landlady. It could have been much worse. It could have been some old hag.

Or a child,' she added thoughtfully. 'Then you would really have something to worry about.' She put the card back in the centre of the pack and smoothed the edges out till all were flush and tidy.

'As it is, you've nothing to be ashamed of.' She stood up and patted me comfortingly on the shoulder. 'An attractive young woman, an eager young man. What could be more natural?' She stooped to bring her mouth level with my ear. 'And you're very well-endowed you know, remarkably well-endowed.' She stroked me lightly on the cheek with her finger-tips and walked briskly out into the street, her jeans clinging to every motion of her swaying buttocks.

Despite her reassurance, I was reluctant to return to the hotel and confront either the landlady or her cuckolded husband. His original offer of her to me, however honestly intended, might have been hedged round with restrictions and limitations that I did not understand, and I had enough evidence, in any case, of his unpredictability to make me unwilling to run any risks with him. Nevertheless, I was hungry and the afternoon stretched dreary and empty before me, with at least six or seven hours to pass before the ceremony of Walking on Water – which I was determined to witness – could begin.

I decided to see if I could pick up something to eat at the hotel, after which I would return to the headland and resume work on the statue. In that way I would be able to keep an eye on the people at the Institute and might even be able to join them for the ritual itself. Meanwhile I could perhaps find out more about the meaning of this event by cautious questioning of the landlady.

Her husband had gone from the hotel doorway and there was no sign of him inside the building. The landlady was in the kitchen, preparing something on the counter. She swirled round quickly when she heard me enter, then relaxed and smiled as she recognised me. 'I've been expecting you,' she said. 'I have something special for lunch.' I thought I detected complicity in her tone, a mutual understanding of some kind, but she made no overt reference to the intimacy we had presumably shared the previous evening. I studied her as she set the table and prepared the dishes for serving: Martina was right, I decided, I had nothing to be ashamed of in having made love to someone as youthful, fresh, and vigorous as this. If anything, I ought to be proud of myself.

She beckoned to me to sit down and placed in front of me a bowl that steamed with delicious fragrance. She seated herself opposite me and leant across the table, propping herself on her elbows with her hands clasped, and beaming at me expectantly.

'What is it?' I asked, drawing up the scent in a long, blissful sigh, and exhaling slowly and appreciatively.

She explained that it was a sort of *bouillabaisse*, made up of lobster, squid, crab, conch, mussels, shrimp, and three or four different kinds of fish. I thought of the squid I had seen being battered to death that morning, but concluded that it was needless sentimentality to allow that to impair my appetite. Nature is less squeamish than humans are and if the creature had not found its way into my bowl, it would most likely have suffered the fate, sooner or later, of being torn apart and devoured alive, in delicious quivering chunks, by some natural predator instead. I took a spoonful and nodded in something close to ecstasy: 'Magnificent!' I breathed.

Ella glowed with delight and her eyes sparkled. 'Eat and enjoy,' she urged me, 'and afterwards we go to bed.'

I could see no objection to this agenda and continued to eat steadily, savouring each mouthful. When the first edge was off my hunger, I relaxed and leaned back in my chair. She pushed a plateful of bread towards me. 'Eat, eat!' she admonished. 'You must grow big and strong.' I felt like a child, or a victim being fattened in preparation for a cannibal feast, but I obeyed and took a slice. This left a gap on the plate and revealed a crudely painted design on its surface; I drew it closer to me and examined it. I had to remove the rest of the bread to make out the total pattern: daubs and splotches of incompatible and badly-mixed colours that nevertheless cohered to form something disturbingly familiar and almost recognisable.

She noticed my interest. 'Ah, you like our seahorse,' she commented approvingly.

Her words completed the circuit of recognition: crude as it was, the design must represent a seahorse, with its slender, deeply ridged body, the coiled tail, the elongated snout, the scaly, dragon-like head, the sunken eyes. And this, in turn, was the shape that Martina, with apparent idle and casual playfulness, had created on the beach that morning.

'Is there a figure like this in the grotto?' I demanded. I regretted the words almost immediately, for a look of terror flashed into her eyes and she shrank away from me.

'What grotto?' she mumbled. 'I don't know what you mean.'

There seemed no alternative but to persist. 'The grotto on the island,' I said gently. 'I know it has a special significance for your people and I don't wish to pry into your secrets. I just thought that there might be something like this inside it.'

She stood up and began to gather in the dishes, less tense now, but fumbling with them and even trying to remove my half-finished bowl of soup. I held on to it, with the result that it oscillated between us for a few seconds, as though forming the centre of a miniature tug-of-war, and some drops of liquid even spilled over on to the wooden surface of the table. Finally she seemed to come to her senses; she relaxed and let go her grip and stood staring at me hesitantly.

I tried to reassure her by changing the subject. 'When was this dish made?' I enquired, turning it round and round and seeking for some clues in the obviously inept workmanship.

'It's a family heirloom,' she told me eagerly. 'The Ellicotts have owned it for centuries. I too am an Ellicott,' she explained proudly. 'I put it out especially for you.'

This clashed so sharply with what Maria had told me that I sat back in my chair in astonishment, thumping both my hands on the table, the spoon still clutched in my right fist, and glared at her with open suspicion. She was obviously startled and offended by this; hastily scooping up whatever crockery and cutlery was within easy reach, she stepped a few paces back from the table and, in a tone that re-established a formal relationship between host and guest, asked if that was all for now.

I nodded.

'Enjoy your meal,' she said coldly. She turned and went into the kitchen, closing the door firmly behind her.

I had little choice, therefore, but to head for the Institute after my meal. A new idea had occurred to me in the meantime, however, as I reflected on what had just happened, for the design of my statue was now obvious to me: it would be a seahorse, towering proudly on the cliff-top, a beacon and landmark to sailors and fishermen, a challenge and cry of defiance on my part against all the forces that had conspired to baffle and frustrate me since my arrival here, a last gesture of independence before my departure (for I was determined that I too would leave within the next two days). I may not have unravelled all the threads, the statue would announce, I may not have penetrated to the heart of the labyrinth, your nets may still hamper me, your flickering obscurities blind me, but I have found one clue at least, I know something after all!

I walked briskly up the road, ignoring the murderous early-afternoon heat, and arrived on the headland panting and soaked with sweat. The materials still lay scattered where I had left them and I regretted now having hurled some of the most durable and substantial elements of my creation into the sea. More than enough remained, however, for my immediate purposes and I set to work in something close to a frenzy, proceeding with blind instinct and yet certain within myself that every twig was going where it should, that every shell had its destined and irrevocable niche.

For what must have been at least an hour, I barely paused, scarcely even bothering to look at what I had created, to examine or correct it. Finally I had to stop, sweat was streaming into my eyes and making it almost impossible for me to see, and my whole body ached from the constant stooping and straightening-up that my task entailed. I stepped back a few paces to contemplate my achievement and only then became aware that I was being watched by three people who had gathered silently on the grass behind me. I had no idea how long they had been there: one was Davers, the other Maria, and the third was 'Ellicott' – not the man I had accosted and questioned in vain a couple of days before, but he who had taken me out in his boat and forced me to catch lobsters with him.

None of them spoke to me, though Maria acknowledged my presence with an almost imperceptible nod. Davers had adopted the pose in which I had last seen him, his chin propped on the thumb and forefinger of his right hand, his right elbow clasped in the palm of his left hand, his feet about twelve inches apart, with the knees slightly bent. A wisp of smoke curled from his pipe and thinned away into the clear air.

'Well?' I demanded aggressively, for their silence was disconcerting and it was clear that none of them would speak first.

The silence lengthened even further. I heard the putter of a motor boat from the sea below us, a voice that shouted instructions of some kind, or a warning. Davers removed his pipe and held it a few inches from his mouth. 'Well, Maria, my dear,' he began, turning to her with a smile, 'what do *you* think?'

'I don't know,' she replied, 'it's obviously *significant*, but in what does the significance *consist*, in which particular quality does it *cohere*, if you catch my meaning, if you take my drift?'

Her jeering and contemptuous tone astonished me. She had been enigmatic before, certainly, had enjoyed my discomfitures and embarrassments, but her attitude had always been teasing and playful rather than openly hostile. I decided to treat her words as a joke, for the time being, and to enter into what I hoped was the spirit of the discussion.

'I've hardly begun it,' I explained, 'so you can't see much in it at present. Just wait a couple of days though, I guarantee you'll be astonished.'

Maria ignored me. She walked slowly round the statue, prodding it critically with her foot now and then. I held my breath, expecting the whole precarious structure to collapse, to crumble, to disintegrate, dissolving (meta-phorically speaking) into a heap of dust and ashes, but miraculously it held firm.

'I don't know much about art,' she said, again in that horrible sneering voice that was not her own at all, 'but I *do* know what I like, and this I don't like.'

'Wait till it's finished,' I suggested, striving to keep up my good-humoured acceptance of her insults. 'You can't judge it from its present state.' I appealed to Davers, who had scarcely moved from his original position, though his pipe was again clamped firmly between his teeth. 'Can you?'

He removed his pipe once more, examined it thought-fully, prodded at something in the bowl with his thumb, cleared his throat. 'It looks to *me*,' he proclaimed, speaking slowly and distinctly, 'like the torso of some gigantic insect or reptile. It looks to me, shall we say, like an unfinished – let me hazard a guess – like an unfinished centipede.'

As if on cue, 'Ellicott', who had said nothing all this time, merely standing twisting his hat uneasily between his fingers and digging the toe of his boot into the ground, blurted out: 'I know a story about a centipede!'

'Do you now?' Davers turned to him calmly, raising his eyebrows with an air of polite though far from over-whelming interest. 'Why don't you tell us all about it, then?'

I felt that I was being set up for some further humilia-tion, that all this had been planned and prepared in advance, but I decided to stick it out to the end. I gazed enquiringly at 'Ellicott'.

'It was when him and I was at school,' he began, jerking his thick, grimy forefinger towards me, but avoiding my eye, 'and we found this huge centipede crawling across the playground. Huge it was, oh, about *so* long – ' He gestured with his hands held about a foot apart. In other circumstances I might have found his attempts at rustic mannerisms and dialect amusing, they were so obviously fake and contrasted so strongly with the blunt straight-forwardness of the man who had whipped me off in his boat a few days previously.

'And just where *was* this school of which you speak?' enquired Davers. 'That is an important factor.'

'India.'

That was true enough: I had spent some early childhood years there before being sent off to boarding-school.

'And?' Davers prompted gently.

'And so we was in the playground, us and the other kids, and we sees this centipede crawling around. And this one – ' he gestured at me, 'says I've got this new knife for Chitirsmas' (the word he used sounded very like that) 'let's see how sharp it is. And he opens it up and starts sawing away at the pore creature.' He wiped away an invisible tear with the back of his dirt-encrusted hand. His words aroused disturbing recollections in me: I re-membered the incident vividly, though it was not I who had possessed the knife, nor had I carried out the attack. Another child had done this and I had tried to stop him, if I remembered correctly. Or had I merely protested in vain? Or had I stood aside and said nothing, done nothing?

Absorbed in these thoughts, I had missed the next stage of 'Ellicott's' story; he had now reached the part where, after a good deal of effort, I had allegedly managed to cut the creature in half and 'all this horrible, yellow, gooey stuff came purring out,' he announced, with con-siderable relish. I wondered if he had really said 'purring' in place of 'pouring', or whether his atrocious accent had mangled the word instead.

Maria had clapped her hand to her mouth in an emphatic gesture of disgust; she turned her head aside as if she were about to vomit. Before she did so, however, she made sure to catch my eye and I was startled to discover an intent, almost pleading gaze fixed on me instead of the earlier mockery. 'Ellicott' was continuing with his story, random details of recrimination and punishment, but he had obviously lost the thread or had not been sufficiently well rehearsed: he stumbled more and more frequently over his words, reversing and distorting them, putting syllables in the wrong place and even producing grotesquely new constructions. He was grinding feebly to a halt and his eyes were appealing desperately to Davers for assistance, when the latter finally intervened.

'That's enough for now, my good man,' he assured him patronisingly. 'We all get the point of what you have told us. Now run along inside and have a drink.' The man literally tugged his forelock in acknowledgement, and shambled off to the gate, his body bowed in what was intended to express overwhelming emotion of some kind, perhaps grief at the pathos of his story or remorse at the fact that he had even witnessed this 'electricity' – by which I assume he intended 'atrocity'.

I was both amused and puzzled by this performance. I had never told anyone of this incident and had certainly not spoken of it to anyone in the village: how, then, could this man have known of it (even referring to it on our very first encounter) and why had Davers set up this absurd recital of it? Perhaps it had formed one of my dreams soon after my arrival, one that I had completely forgotten, and someone, either one of the villagers or, more likely, Daniels and his friends, had plucked it out and stored it away? Or perhaps my soul, on one of its nocturnal rambles, had spoken about it to 'Ellicott's' soul, in a spirit of conviviality and openness? I smiled, realising that I was rapidly becoming as irrational as the villagers themselves; there must be some other explanation, though I had a sudden, disturbing visual image, almost a snapshot, of a group posed round the dismembered body of a centipede, grinning at the camera, a child – myself – clutching an open clasp-knife firmly in his right fist, a dozen other boys around him, gazing at him admiringly, 'Ellicott' part of the picture too, squatting beside them, baring his yellow, pointed teeth at the camera, reducing himself to their height. It was only a few seconds later, as the image began to fade, that I realised that all the children, myself included, were dressed in shabby black suits and wore tiny black hats that perched unsteadily on their heads.

I discovered with a start that Maria was talking to me and I gazed at her in confusion. 'So you see,' she repeated impatiently, 'we can't have you commemorating an incident of that kind on our property. You'd better leave right away.'

'Leave?' I muttered, still dazed by the intensity of the image I had just experienced.

'Yes, leave!' She stamped her foot angrily on the grass. 'Go away from here, go away from the village. Leave right away. Go tonight.' I caught another of those solemn, intense glances: 'Leave,' it seemed to be saying, 'but for your own good, before something happens that you cannot foresee, that you cannot control. I wish you well, I care for you, and I want you to leave.'

'I can't go tonight,' I protested. 'Not before the Walking on Water. I've got to see that. After that, I'll go.'

She threw up her hands in a gesture of despair and

strode off. I hesitated, glancing at Davers for assistance, but he ignored me, staring intently at the statue and puffing on his pipe.

I set off after Maria, but by the time I reached the gate, she had already entered and the main door was just closing behind her. I thought of ringing the bell, but decided I had better come to terms with the afternoon's events before becoming more deeply – and bewilderingly – involved. I walked off slowly down the path and, after about fifty yards, I heard the scuffle of feet behind me. I whirled round, my heart jumping at the prospect of finding that Maria had followed me after all, but it was only 'Ellicott', a huge grin on his face, striding jauntily along and whistling through his teeth.

'Lovely day,' he greeted me, as though we had only just met and the incidents of the last hour had never taken place. He glanced critically up at the cloudless sky. 'It'll be a grand night for the Walking.'

He had fallen into step beside me and, as he turned to look at me, I caught the reek of alcohol on his breath. 'You can come with me in my boat, if you want. I take you cheap.'

I stared at him in fascinated disgust. He had lost all trace of his earlier hesitation and awkwardness; he was self-confident, even arrogant, once again. 'I'm not interested,' I said shortly. I quickened my pace, hoping to shake him off, but he calmly lengthened his stride to keep up with me.

'You need a boat,' he assured me. 'You see nothing from the shore.'

This was probably true enough, but I had no desire to enrich or accommodate him in any way after the performance I had just witnessed. It should be easy enough to find someone else to take me. 'I'm not interested,' I repeated, 'and, what's more, I don't want you walking beside me.' I stopped short, without warning, with the result that his own momentum carried him a few paces past me before he could come to a halt. He glanced back at me quizzically. 'It's your choice,' he acknowledged. I sat down by the roadside and watched till he had dwindled to a faint speck, a caterpillar humping along the dusty road, before I rose slowly to my feet and followed him.

Though I was determined not to accept his offer, I realised that I ought to hire a boat for the evening if I was to have a proper view of the ceremony, and the obvious place to look for someone to take me was in the tavern. To my delight, almost the first person I saw when I entered was Hanslett, the man who had warned me against Ellicott and who had seemingly vanished from sight after explaining the principles of Seahorse to me in my hotel room. I pushed my way towards him through the crowd (for the place was unusually full and there was a general air of tense anticipation, no doubt directed towards the events in store for the evening), seized him by the elbow and offered to buy him a drink.

He acknowledged my presence with a curt nod and continued the conversation that I had interrupted. I waited patiently for him to finish, meanwhile ordering two glasses of the local red wine. Finally he turned back towards me, emptied his glass at a gulp, and asked what I wanted. I said that I planned to watch the ceremony that night and could he take me with him in his boat? He agreed easily enough and said he would be leaving just before dark, at eight o'clock. He pushed his glass back across the bar and signalled to the girl to fill it up again. Once more he drained it at one draught.

In an attempt at conviviality, for he had fixed me with

a somewhat disconcerting stare, I said that I had learned a lot more about Seahorse since I had last seen him. 'Though I can't claim to *understand* it any better,' I admitted. He nodded thoughtfully and ordered some more wine, this time savouring it more slowly and resting the glass on the counter half-full. 'And I've been dreaming too,' I continued, hoping to elicit a more positive response from him and finding that his silence forced me to be much more voluble than I had originally intended. 'Such strange dreams they were. If I told you about them, you wouldn't suspect me any longer of causing dreams in the village. I'm as much a victim as you are.'

He nodded again and finished his drink. He signalled to the girl to bring some more. I wondered if I was expected to pay for all this and was rapidly calculating the amount of spare change in my pocket when my attention was drawn to an argument at one of the nearby tables. Someone had laid a Seahorse card face upwards in the centre of the table: it had, I gathered, been added to the pack only very recently, and a lively debate was under way as to how to name it.

Hanslett elbowed his way through the crowd, attracting a few scowls and even one or two blows as he did so, and I squeezed apologetically in his wake, entering the gap he had opened up before it had time to close and reform once more. I found that I could peer easily over the heads of those in the row before me and I suddenly knew, before I had even glimpsed it, what the card would represent: the figure of Idi Amin in the posture that had closed my dream, standing with his hands on his hips, beaming warmly into the camera.

A babble of attempted identification arose around me: the most popular guess was that it was 'Good Old Uncle Joe' Stalin, while others claimed that it was 'Winnie'

Churchill, the gallant airman who had won the war single-handed in aerial combat with the dragon Adolf. The man's skin colour puzzled adherents of both parties, however, as well as those on the fringes who were offering 'Alec Ike', Napoleon, or – more daringly up-to-date – Fidel Castro, and there was an air of uncertainty and confusion about the whole discussion that threatened to sink it in a morass of futile recrimination.

Secure in my superior knowledge, I offered – somewhat smugly, and as it turned out, unwisely – to arbitrate, and told them who the picture really depicted. All stared at me uncomprehendingly, several with a scornful smile flickering at the corner of their mouths, and a few even tapped their foreheads significantly and nodded wisely to their cronies. I attempted to explain further, but found myself floundering in a mounting wave of incredulity and hostility and finally Hanslett himself cut me short: 'It's *Good Old Uncle Joe*,' he maintained firmly, and the others, accepting his decision without further argument, continued with their game.

Flushed with embarrassment, I eased my way back through the crowd, certain that all were enjoying my discomfiture, though in fact few people even glanced at me and all were drifting back to their previous occupations. Once I was outside, I set off straight back for the hotel, determined to rest for a few hours before confronting whatever new ordeal the night might bring me.

I threw myself on to my bed and fell almost immediately into an uneasy sleep, rousing myself intermittently under the impression that the landlord was standing by my bedside, demanding immediate payment for several hundred barrels of wine consumed by Hanslett at my expense. Each time I returned more soundly to sleep and it was only under much protest and after many struggles that I at last acknowledged that someone was indeed shaking me vigorously by the shoulder and urging me to get up.

It was Hanslett who was standing beside my bed, his face dark with anger. 'It's late!' he hissed. 'It's after eight o'clock. We'll ruin everything if you don't hurry!'

I pulled on my sandals and stumbled blearily towards the door, thanking him profusely for taking the trouble to search for me. I wanted to reach for a sweater, anticipating that the night would be chilly, but he seized me impatiently by the elbow and hustled me down the stairs and into the deserted streets. The moon floated high above us, serene in a cloudless sky; I was given little opportunity to contemplate it, though, as Hanslett dragged me down the steps and across the beach to his boat.

All the other boats had left the shore already and were heading towards a gathering place about halfway to the island, where they joined a roughly circular formation, each boat illuminated by a lamp placed in its prow. From there a row of lights about a hundred yards apart signalled the position of half a dozen other boats, those carrying the children who, as I had been led to believe, would walk in relay to the island. I wondered once again how this feat could be performed, or rather by what trickery the impression of it was created. Perhaps some kind of mass hallucination was at work, encouraged by drugs or some species of religious ecstasy (though, despite the existence of the church and its remarkably well-preserved condition, I had seen no evidence anywhere of a priest or of any services being conducted there). More likely, each child would be lowered on to the surface of the water for a few seconds, as a symbolic gesture, and then either escorted to the rendezvous, supported, from within the boat, by a parent; or simply rowed there once the token ritual had been fulfilled.

I suggested something of this to Hanslett, but my words must have been drowned by the droning of his outboard motor, or carried away by the wind, for he made no response other than to scowl at me as though I was distracting him from some more important concern. We reached the waiting boats and took our place in the circle; as if this was a signal for the ceremony to begin, a man rose to his feet in a boat positioned exactly in the centre and launched into a recital of an obviously prepared speech. Under the circumstances, for the wind had risen and the boats were pitching on the waves in an increasingly alarming manner, I could make out little of this, but what I could hear seemed to be in an archaic and almost incomprehensible version of the village language.

The formula must have been familiar enough to the listeners, however, for no one was paying much attention and whispered conversations were taking place between neighbouring boats. I gathered that Hanslett was being reproached for his late arrival and for having forced everyone to wait for him : presumably everyone in the village, even strangers and visitors like myself, had to be present if the ceremony was to be successful.

I suddenly realised that the boat two places away to my left was occupied by the people from the Institute: Davers was there, and Maria and also Martina, and Ellicott sat grimly at the helm. It was not their own boat, the one I had seen them in a few nights previously, and there was no sign either of Dr Daniels. I assumed that he must be there somewhere, if my conclusion that *everyone* had to attend the event was correct, but, though I looked carefully in all the other boats nearby, I could see no sign of him.

Meanwhile Davers had caught sight of me and had made the two women aware of my presence. Rising clumsily to his feet, causing the boat to rock and plunge violently as he did so, he made an elaborate mock bow: 'Good evening, Mr Over-ripe, so nice to have you with us.' His voice floated eerily across the water, like some disembodied spirit.

Maria giggled. 'It's not *Over*-ripe, silly,' she corrected him. 'It's *Ever*-ripe.'

I sent her a glance full of hurt reproach that I hoped would cause her at least a momentary blush of shame, but she paid no attention. She reached up to Davers and drew him to sit down beside her; her arm went round his shoulders and she cuddled close to him. Automatically, I looked over at Martina to see how she would take this; she appeared unconcerned by it and was concentrating on the speaker, who was still droning away in the centre of the assembly.

Davers shrugged himself free of Maria's embrace and reached for something in his pocket. He took out a notebook and a pen and fiddled with the latter for a few seconds until a thin, clear beam of light could be seen from the tip. He began to write busily, glancing occasionally at the speaker, and obviously taking down his words.

Though I had left my jacket in my room and so could not verify my suspicion, I knew, with absolute certainty, that it was *my* pen that he was using. I could not imagine how he had got hold of it, unless one of the women had somehow appropriated it for him when she was in my company. Resentment at their contemptuous treatment of me combined with an atavistic and involuntary impulse to defend my possessions at all costs, and I called over to him angrily: 'Where did you get that pen? Give it back to me!'

Davers raised his head and turned slowly to look at me. He smiled and then went on with his writing. His coolness infuriated me even more: 'Give it back, I tell you,' I yelled, 'or else you'll regret it!' I rose to my feet, ignoring the swaying of the boat and a startled grunt of alarm from Hanslett. 'Give it back!' I even shook my fist at him.

Davers closed his notebook and returned it to his pocket. 'Nothing much new. Much the same as always,' he remarked to his companions. The orator, I realised, had finally come to a halt; he was sitting once more in the prow of his boat and a gap was widening out in the boats ahead of him to allow him passage. A small boy was now standing by his side and the man had placed his hand reassuringly on his shoulder.

'Give me my pen!' I repeated angrily, as the other boats prepared to move ahead and keep pace with him. I no longer expected my pleas to have any effect and I was therefore taken by surprise when Davers, without even looking in my direction, tossed the pen casually into the air, over the heads of the people in the intervening boat, and towards me. He had left it lit, and the beam moved in a slow trajectory, a graceful and almost perfect arc, that I gazed at as if spellbound. When I moved, scrambling a couple of feet along the side of the boat in an attempt to catch it, I was just fractionally too late: the object touched the water a bare inch beyond my reach, almost grazing my outstretched fingers, and I had the mortification of seeing it sink, slowly at first and then with increasing rapidity, into the murky waters, its light leading my gaze irresistibly down with it into the depths.

I jerked my head away from its hypnotic lure and glared at Davers, but his boat was underway now and all those in it seemed to have lost interest in me. Hanslett had re-started the engine and we were moving too, into a new alignment that brought all the boats into a straight line, with that containing the orator and the child exactly in the centre. As soon as this new pattern was achieved, the orator stood up once more, muttered a few words into the child's ear, seized him firmly under the armpits, swung him over the side of the boat, deposited him gently on the water, and released him.

I expected the boy to resist or struggle, to panic as so many of the children had done during the preparations for this moment at the fountain, but he moved calmly and serenely ahead, setting one foot before the other as confidently as if he were doing nothing more remarkable than setting off down the street to buy a loaf of bread. The boats edged slowly forward, keeping pace with him and, once he had gone about ten yards, he acknowledged our presence by smiling cheerfully to right and left, nodding his head, and even waving to members of his family or particular friends. I had assumed immediately that some kind of hypnotism was at work, to give him the confidence to make the venture at all; but his easy, relaxed manner was totally at variance with the vacant, trance-like state of someone in that condition.

He soon reached the next stage, where he was lifted gently into the waiting boat and a small girl took his place. She too gave no sign of fear or apprehension and, in fact, scampered along so rapidly that it was all we could do to keep level with her. All the engines had been switched off once the Walk had actually begun, and there was complete silence save for the regular dip and splash of oars, the slow taking-in and exhalation of breath.

A third child took his turn, then a fourth and fifth. The wind had risen in force and was chopping at the waves, driving them to slap with increasing vehemence against the side of the boat. I noticed that Hanslett and some of the others were glancing anxiously at the children and then at the shore ahead of them, calculating the distance yet to be covered; someone uttered a cry of anxiety and pointed up at the sky, where a dark cloud had appeared from nowhere and was scurrying rapidly towards the moon.

The fifth stretch was almost completed and the boy was being urged on with hoarse cries of encouragement. He was obviously infected by the mood of anxiety and clumsily attempted to run, pumping his little feet down on the uneven surface of the water, soaking himself in the process and once or twice stumbling and only barely preventing himself from falling flat. At last he arrived at the boat and was pulled eagerly inside; the final participant, a girl once again, was lowered hastily into the water, but, even as this happened, an almost universal groan arose from the villagers, for the cloud was now within easy reach of the moon and would certainly obscure it before she could gain the shore. Hanslett stopped rowing and rested his hands on his lap, the blades of the oars standing high in the air, streaming with droplets that glinted and sparkled in the moonbeams. 'It's no use,' he muttered. 'She'll never make it.'

Meanwhile the child had pulled herself free of the hands that, prematurely anticipating defeat, had hesitated to release her; she too began to run across the water, but so lightly that her feet barely skimmed the surface and I could have sworn at times that they did not touch it at all and she was running completely on air. Even this, however, was not going to be sufficient: the cloud had touched the edge of the moon and, in a few moments more, would obscure it completely. I looked back at the girl and saw that she was now actually *flying* towards the shore, suspended a good four feet above the waves as if held there by wires from an invisible helicopter overhead. A gasp of astonishment from the villagers confirmed my belief that something unusual had indeed taken place; she raised her right hand in a gesture of triumph and swooped down towards the beach, her feet touching the ground at the very moment that the cloud blotted out the last ray of moonlight.

There was a huge sigh of relief from the watchers, the sound rippling and flowing from boat to boat, then breaking up into an excited clatter of voices, laughter, shouts, and even applause. I looked across at the boat from the Institute: Davers had risen to his feet once again and was pointing excitedly at the shore; he stood firm and rock-steady this time, defying the pitching of the boat. 'Maria!' he gloated, 'Martina! Did you see that? My God, that *is* unusual! It was worth coming here just for that.'

The cloud was moving away from the moon again and a dramatic finger of light had found the little girl as she stood on the beach, isolating her against the blackness of the island as if she stood on stage. There was a burst of cheering, wild cries of delight, and a surge forward as those boats that had originally contained the children made for the shore. Hanslett, however, held back, as did the majority of the vessels; presumably only a privileged few were allowed actually to set foot on the island, even on an occasion such as this.

I heard a splash close by and turned to see a large black animal, about the size of a dog, that had just jumped into the water from the boat containing Davers and the two women. It must have been lying concealed there all this time and I expected Davers to call it back or to try to recover it. He paid no attention, however, and none of the villagers seemed to have noticed it. It swam powerfully towards the shore, its flat head with the long, pointed muzzle only partly visible, the jaws apart and the white teeth glinting in the moonlight. It reached the sand, shook itself dry, and loped off in the direction of the tower, without a backward glance. Something about it reminded me of the animal that had flown at me from its kennel and attempted to savage me, yet there was also an aspect of it that did not quite match with this, that remained both determinedly obscure and naggingly familiar.

The boats had now been pulled up on to the shore and the six children had been gathered together in a group. The man who had delivered the oration took charge and, together with about a dozen adults, who I assumed were the children's parents, moved them off in a procession in the direction of the tower. The remaining adults, who must have acted purely as boatmen, squatted on the sand in a circle to await their return.

Hanslett now began to manoeuvre his boat to face away from the island and I saw that the others were doing the same. He stored the oars away and moved to start the engine up once again. It burst into life almost simultaneously with those of the other boats and he steered us rapidly back to the mainland, bumping and jolting over the uneven waves with a force that sometimes took my breath away. When we reached land, I asked him what he wanted in payment; he shrugged and said I could buy him a few drinks.

We walked slowly up the steps and, when we reached the top, I paused to look back over the beach. We had been almost the first to arrive and the moonlit sand was now dotted irregularly with the black shapes of men and women, usually in isolated groups of two or three, but gradually drifting together and forming larger concentrations as they neared the steps.

Hanslett tugged impatiently at my sleeve. 'Hurry,' he urged me. 'Tonight *everyone* will be at the bar. We must be quick or else we wait all night.'

We walked swiftly to the tavern, where we found that the landlord had arrived before us and was happily arranging barrels and bottles of wine in anticipation of a profitable evening. He greeted us cordially and poured out two glasses even before being asked. 'Who would have thought it,' he wheezed confidently to Hanslett, helping himself to a drink as well, 'that a Lincott could do something like that?' Hanslett grunted noncommittally, and turned his back on him to survey the customers who were rapidly filling up the room, chattering and laughing excitedly. The landlord was soon too busy to have further time for us, and Hanslett, muttering a word of excuse, went off to talk to one of his cronies.

I remained leaning against the bar, taking an occasional sip from my glass, and surveying the scene around me. Rather unusually, the crowd was composed almost equally of men and women; and I even noticed several women among those who had secured a table early and were now engrossed in games of Seahorse – a sight I was certain I had never witnessed before. I ordered another drink from the waitress – the landlord was bustling obsequiously around the room, oozing affability and goodwill – and wondered if anything else was planned or if the main excitement of the evening was over.

Each time the landlord passed near me I heard him commenting, in feigned wonderment, on the fact that the child who had flown to the shore had been a *Lincott*. I remembered Martina's comment that the Ellicotts had only recently risen in the estimation of the villagers and that the Lincotts now occupied the bottom rank in the local hierarchy; doubtless the landlord felt insecure in his new status and was subtly trying to denigrate his potential rivals. His fat face was steaming with sweat and he became more reckless and outspoken as the evening went on: 'Lincotts,' I heard him say contemptuously to someone at a table close to me, 'they're not fit to step inside the tower. They even pollute it by farting a mile away, if the wind is in the right direction.'

A man rose to his feet at the table behind him, overturning his chair with a clatter. He grabbed the landlord by the grimy collar of his soiled shirt and whirled him round to face him. The glasses which he was carrying spilled off the tray and shattered on the floor; the noise brought instant silence to the room and even those playing Seahorse paused to watch what was happening.

Realising who was holding him, the landlord whitened with terror and began to babble incoherent apologies: 'I'm sorry, Mr Lincott, sir, I didn't mean it, Mr Lincott, it was just a joke not to be taken seriously, sir, please forgive me.' He was by now almost on his knees and, dropping the tray that he had continued to clutch, he clasped his hands pathetically together, and peered upwards theatrically as if begging for mercy. His assailant dragged him to his feet, stared into his eyes for a few seconds, then tossed him contemptuously aside and resumed his seat.

The landlord bent down to pick up the tray and, straightening up, he smirked and winked confidentially at some of his friends nearby. 'Lincotts!' he mouthed silently and made a gesture as if of spitting. He had been too incautious, however, not realising that Lincott had continued to watch him after sitting down. Infuriated beyond endurance, the man leapt to his feet once more, seized a wine bottle that was standing on the table, and brought it down on the landlord's head with a sickening thud. The bottle smashed to pieces and a trickle of red liquid ran down the man's neck; to my astonishment, though he staggered a little, he showed no other sign of distress. He merely shook his head slowly and emphatically from side to side two or three times, and went off behind the bar without even looking at his attacker. Lincott stood for a moment, staring after him, with the neck of the broken bottle still clutched in his hand and dangling by his side; finally he tossed this on to the floor and sat down again. He said nothing to his companions and appeared to be deep in thought.

The normal activities of the tavern gradually resumed and the incident appeared to have been forgotten. The landlord returned with a fresh tray of drinks, a bandage fastened round the top of his head; he was more subdued than previously and he was careful to give a wide berth to the area where Lincott was sitting, allowing the waitress to serve the orders for that group. I felt in need of fresh air and then sleep; Hanslett was nowhere to be seen and I told myself that I had done my best to discharge my obligation to him and had no need to seek him out and ply him with more drinks.

I eased my way through the crowd and out into the cool night air. As this might well be my last evening in the village, I decided to take a final walk in the direction of the Institute, savouring the beauty of the evening and the quietness of the landscape. As I passed the church, I realised, with some irritation at my own obtuseness, that I ought to have arranged with Hanslett while I had the opportunity, that I would hire his boat to take me away the next morning. I almost turned back to search for him again, but decided that it was probably useless and that, in any case, almost any of the other fishermen would welcome the payment I could offer.

The moonlight cast long shadows across the path from the trees and bushes on either side of the road. The solitary cloud had long since vanished and the moon rode high and clear in the sky, dappled with the dark patches of its seas and mountains. I thought of the astronauts who had walked there and wondered if anyone in the village knew or cared about this, whether they would believe me if I told them and whether they would counter with some fantastic and ridiculous assertion of their own, beyond all bounds of reason and logic. They would tell me perhaps that, in the old days, their souls used to go on vacation there, gallivanting wildly and freely, sliding up and down the path of moonbeams. . . .

I turned a bend in the road and almost collided with two figures walking in close embrace, arms twined tenderly around each other. I jerked away, mumbling an apology, and began to circle round them; one of them stretched out an arm to detain me. 'Don't go just yet,' she said, in that cool, slightly mocking voice I had come to know so well. 'We might not see each other again.'

I recognised Martina and, beside her, still clutching her affectionately, Maria. Both smiled at the confusion that must have registered on my features, but offered no explanation of their presence or their relationship. 'It's a beautiful night,' Martina went on, arching back her head to look up at the moon. The gesture, no doubt deliberately, had the effect of thrusting her breasts forward so that they were tautly outlined against her thin blouse.

'Are you leaving tomorrow?' I asked.

'Yes.'

I glanced at Maria for confirmation, and she nodded almost imperceptibly.

'And you've completed your work here?' I suggested.

'Have *you?*' It was Maria who spoke, countering a question with another question, as always.

'I think so.'

'That's good.' There was a pause. I shifted my weight from one foot to the other, uncertain how and when to take my leave.

'Will you be back again?' I asked.

'Will *you?*'

'I don't know. It all depends.' I looked away from them, towards the headland and the Institute, where the fragment of my statue was sharply outlined against the pale sky. Maria followed my gaze.

'It's a pity you didn't finish that,' she murmured. 'It's the one thing we've left incomplete.'

I was about to say that I had received very little encouragement to continue with it on the last occasion, but decided to hold my peace.

'It would be nice to have it completed,' she persisted, musing more to herself than to me. 'Why can't you stay just a day longer and finish it?'

I gave up trying to understand her: one day she was urging me to leave, the next begging me to stay. 'I've got more important things to do,' I replied shortly.

'Oh, your book,' she murmured vaguely.

'Yes, my book. And other things,' I added, driven once again by that urge I always felt in her presence to come closer to the truth than I had originally intended.

'I would have thought this was an ideal place for writing,' Martina broke in. 'Peaceful, romantic, exotic. Have you been to see the mermaid yet?' she added unexpectedly.

I thought I detected a chuckle from Maria, that she instantly turned into a clearing of the throat. 'Oh, yes, the mermaid,' she said solemnly. 'You can't leave without talking to the mermaid.'

I had had enough of this foolishness: their incomprehensible and unmotivated mockery was grating on my nerves. 'I have to go now,' I said, with as much dignity as I could muster. 'It's been nice talking to you. I hope we meet again sometime.'

'I'm sure we will,' Maria answered politely. She drew her arm closer round Martina's waist and snuggled her head on her shoulder. 'I'm so tired,' she yawned. 'It's been a hard night.'

'And it's so hot,' Martina moaned. Both of them seemed to have forgotten me and I hesitated, hoping for some acknowledgement from Martina, a word of farewell at least. 'Undo my blouse for me, will you?' she asked Maria, 'I desperately need some air.'

Maria undid one button, then another. She slipped her hand inside the blouse and began to caress the other woman's breast. Both had their eyes closed and breathed deeply, ecstatically.

I turned abruptly on my heel and left them, expecting to be pursued by groans of simulated delight, interrupted perhaps by stifled giggles, but the night was totally silent once again. I strode on down the road, irritated at my passivity, my acceptance of the obscurity with which Davers and the two women had chosen to surround themselves. I tried to persuade myself that more determination on my part, a refusal to be put off so easily by their evasive and elliptical remarks, would have given me some clue as to their real purpose here and the nature of their interaction with the villagers; yet I knew all along that I had made this attempt often enough, and failed.

A long, low howling came from somewhere behind

me, a weird, uncanny sound that stopped me in my tracks and made me look around, shivering, for its source. It came once again, from the direction of the Institute, and, peering through a gap in the trees that shielded the building from view, I detected something squatting beside my statue that had not been there a few minutes previously. The animal – for it could be nothing else – raised its head towards the sinking moon and bayed mournfully. I thought of the dog that had jumped out of Ellicott's boat and had headed for the island, but it could scarcely have swum the mile back on its own, and that boat, I had particularly remarked, had returned to the mainland with the others.

The creature had changed position: it was now standing on its hind legs with its forepaws hunched over my statue, as if embracing it. Once again it lifted its head and howled at the moon. The sound echoed through the deserted landscape, chilling me, and making me look uneasily around for shapes lurking in the bushes, unseen dangers ready to pounce. I searched for the beast again: it had now moved away from the statue and was prancing unsteadily about on its hind feet, like some grotesque human parody; after a few moments it dropped back on all fours and loped swiftly out of sight, behind the trees.

I became irrationally convinced that it was coming in my direction, scampering down the path with teeth bared, and – for the second time within a week – I found myself walking with forced and measured haste towards the safety of the village. I made myself stop now and then to look behind me and listen carefully for pattering feet; to my relief the night continued as silent as ever and I gradually relaxed as I reached the outlying buildings and finally sauntered nonchalantly through the empty streets to the hotel with my hands stuck casually in my pockets.

I lit the oil lamp as soon as I entered my room and prepared to get at least a little sleep before my departure. As I undressed I became aware that something was wrong in the room, something was out of place or missing, or an unfamiliar element had been introduced. It was some time before I tracked this down to the fact that the covering had not merely been removed from the mirror, but had been discarded completely and was nowhere to be found. Not that it matters, I thought, at this stage, and I raised the lamp in my right hand to head height to examine myself and to discern, if possible, what changes had been brought about in my appearance by the events of the past few days. My face might be lined with wrinkles, I mused sardonically, my hair turned grey, I would scarcely recognise the face that peered back at me through the smeared and fly-specked glass.

The lamp winked back at itself, floating high in the air, remote and unsupported. It threw a circle of light that outlined some of the objects behind me in the room, the foot of the bed, the rickety chair, the corner of the partition that walled off the bathroom. Of myself there was nothing to be seen, a vacancy only, a serene disembodiment, that persisted for a few brief seconds before the lamp began to tremble violently, plunging, of its own accord it seemed, to the floor, to be immediately extinguished.

I slept little that night, huddling under the bedclothes and shivering uncontrollably. I had better leave at once, I thought, before worse could happen to me, though I could scarcely imagine what worse than this could occur. I had better stay then, I decided, and try to salvage what I could from the situation, find out who had done this to me and try to negotiate some compromise that would return my reflection, or my soul, or whatever it was that had been taken from me. I could come to no final resolution, shifting from one alternative to the other, and finally I dozed off shortly after dawn, waking with a start less than an hour later as a tremendous groan reverberated through the house, a sound of sheer agony and terror that brought me bolt upright in my bed, staring wildly around me. Though I listened carefully, I could hear nothing else: the house was totally still and from the street came only the quiet flap of sandals on the cobbles as some early risers set about the day's business.

Inadequate as it was, my sleep had calmed me down to some extent: what had happened to me was strange, certainly, but it could not be totally inexplicable. Some trickery must be at work, I realised, as with the other mysterious events of my visit, and the quartet at the Institute, in collusion doubtless with some of the villagers, must be responsible. My first priority, then, must be to intercept them before they could leave the area, force a confrontation, and wrest an explanation from them, by force if necessary.

I scrambled out of bed, narrowly avoiding placing my foot on one of the fragments of glass from the broken oil lamp. I picked my way through these to the mirror and stood before it, leaning on the surface of the dressing-table with my knuckles taking the weight of my body, bending forward till my forehead almost touched the glass. I could see the room behind me clearly, every detail sharply outlined by the early morning sunlight, but there was still no trace of myself. Yet my breath formed a brief circle of condensation on the glass before me, and when I raised my right hand and pressed it firmly on the surface, it too left a trace behind that lingered for several seconds before dissolving.

I straightened up and took a pace backwards: there must be some peculiarity in the glass that caused this illusion, or perhaps some elaborate deception was involved, with multiple mirrors placed at carefully chosen angles to cancel each other out. I remembered films where the camera seemed to be placed directly in front of a mirror and yet could not itself be seen; something of the same kind must be at work here. At any rate, I had no time to puzzle it out just now; I dressed rapidly, splashed some water on my face, and headed out into the street.

I stopped to buy some of the local variety of croissant at the baker's and began to eat one as I walked past the silent, empty church with its crenellated, stalagmite-shaped towers, then strode away from the village and up the path to the Institute. Even this early in the morning, it was uncomfortably warm and promised to be one of the hottest days I had experienced since my arrival. Instead of slowing down, however, I quickened my pace and, by the time I reached the headland, I was almost running. I grabbed hold of the bell rope sharply and tugged on it violently; I could hear the sound reverberate faintly within the walls and I leaned against the wall, panting and trying to overcome the thick, choking sensation in my throat.

There was no sound from within. I pulled the rope sharply again and this time the bell jangled loudly inside. When even this produced no response, I rang again and again, allowing no respite, till it seemed that the sound filled the whole landscape and might even be heard in the village. At last I was forced to stop: my arm ached and my whole body was shaking, my eyes refused to focus properly any longer and the walls of the Institute danced and shifted before me in impudent mockery.

I gave up and moved on to where the statue stood. I

noticed that the grass around it had recently been trampled flat, though the earth was too dry to distinguish footprints or pawmarks. As I stood uncertainly beside it, trying to determine my next move, I heard the familiar sound of the boat belonging to the Institute. I rushed to the edge of the cliff and peered over: they were about a hundred yards out from shore and heading out to sea, Dr Daniels, as before, at the helm, his mane of silver hair streaming out behind him, the two women lounging in the stern, and Davers occupying himself with something in the prow.

I yelled to them to stop, that I had something urgent to tell them; I jumped up and down on the cliff-top, waving my arms. Only Maria seemed to notice me: she waved back, in a gesture either of comradeship or of mockery, and called something. The words were snatched away from me by the wind, but I thought they sounded like: 'See you next year!'

Dr Daniels began to sing. His deep bass voice carried powerfully to the shore and once again it was an old sea song: 'What Shall We Do With The Drunken Sailor?' He sang with zest and gusto, raising his right hand from the steering-wheel to beat time; the others joined in the chorus, flinging it out with equal enthusiasm and with what I imagined – no doubt erroneously – to be particular reference to myself.

I retained a faint hope that the boat might be making for the island and would return later in the day, but I had to relinquish this when I saw it set a course that would take it well to the right and into the open sea instead. I watched nevertheless, my eyes straining to follow them as the boat dwindled to a black speck on the grey-green, heaving ocean; they persisted with their song to the very end too, so that the words floated back to me for what seemed like hours: 'Put him in the longboat till he's sober, Put him in the longboat till he's sober, Put him in the longboat till he's sober, Ear-lie in the morning!'

A sudden gust of wind buffeted the statue beside me, jangling some of its elements together, metal against stone, shell grating against shell, the cheap necklaces and trinkets tinkling as they twisted slowly in the breeze. Seized by a blind impulse of rage, I flung myself at it kicking out wildly with my feet and tugging randomly at its materials with my hands. To my astonishment, it stood firm, resisting my assault so completely that the only element I could detach was the old gramophone record that had formed part of Davers' original structure. I glanced at the title: 'Selected Sea Shanties, sung by Damon Daniels to his own accompaniment'. I smashed it to pieces across my knee and hurled it as far as I could over the cliff, in the direction of the now invisible boat.

There was nothing for it but to return to the village. I took a final look at the gloomy, impenetrable building, whose secrets I would now never uncover, and set off down the path, every inch of whose uneven surface I had come to know and detest intimately. On either side of me birds sang cheerfully, welcoming the new day; insects buzzed and chirped in the grass; even the dull boom of the sea against the rocks at the foot of the cliff was audible. I would pack and leave after all: once I had shaken off the atmosphere of the region, once I was free of the delusive spells cast by the villagers, everything would fall into place once more, normality would reassert itself.

I walked rapidly through the village, brushing past the inhabitants without a word of apology, ignoring the stares and the muttered reproaches. I would get the landlady to recommend someone reliable to take me away immediately, at whatever price he might demand. I flung open the main door to the hotel and strode into the foyer, calling her name loudly. When there was no answer, I entered the dining-room and saw the landlord seated at a table with his back turned to me, slumped forward as if in a drunken stupor; his head faced away from me, and thick folds of skin creased the back of his neck.

I was about to seize him by the shoulder and shake him roughly awake, when I realised that a large carving-knife protruded from his back, just below the neck and towards the right shoulder. He had bled freely at first – like a stuck pig I thought irrelevantly – but the blood had already caked and congealed around the wound, and he must have been dead for several hours. I lifted his arm to feel his pulse nevertheless; he had been working on some documents when he was stabbed, his business accounts no doubt, and some of these had been caught beneath his body, while others had been knocked to the floor as he fell forward. As I raised his arm, a piece of paper came with it; after a few seconds it detached itself and fluttered towards the floor, drifting and swirling endlessly before it finally settled.

There was a faint scraping sound from the direction of the kitchen door and I whirled round, releasing the arm so that it fell with a dull thump on the table once more. The landlady stood in the doorway, her eyes unnaturally bright, a faint half-smile on her lips. 'I did it for you,' she said. She came towards me, with arms outstretched as if to embrace me, and I backed away wildly, squeezing myself into the far corner of the room. She must be mad, I thought, trying to calculate how best to reach the door, for she blocked off direct access to it.

'I did it for you,' she repeated, with a look of puzzlement on her face now and a hurt tone to her voice. 'Don't you want me?' I nodded, intent merely on pacifying her and then eluding her once her tense scrutiny of me relaxed. 'That's good,' she said. She came close to me, smiling once more, her right hand stretched towards my shoulder. I twitched away from her involuntarily, but she secured me and brought me closer to her. 'I always knew you wanted it this way,' she whispered in my ear, nibbling me playfully with her sharp teeth. She closed them unexpectedly in a quick bite and laughed as I jerked away from her with a yelp. 'Now we go to bed,' she suggested.

I stared at the dead man slumped at the table not three feet away from me. I could see his face now, contorted with pain, the lips drawn back to bare the jagged, uneven, decaying teeth. I remembered the groan of agony I had heard earlier that morning. 'Don't worry about him.' She spoke with revulsion, following my gaze. 'No one will regret him. Everyone hated him in the vaillage. He is better off dead.'

'But what will you do?' I asked. My mind was so confused that I could think no further ahead than the next step in the immediate situation. 'Won't you be arrested? And I have to leave this morning,' I added suddenly, remembering my recent decision and looking round the room as if expecting to find my suitcase propped in the doorway, neatly packed, and a taxi-driver waiting for me cap in hand.

'You won't leave,' she assured me confidently. She had put her arms around me once again and was nibbling my ear-lobe tenderly. There was the smell of garlic on her breath; it had always been there, I realised. 'And I don't understand what you mean, "arrested".'

'Prison,' I explained. 'Locked up.'

She shook her head. 'All that will happen is that I will

stand at the crossroads for three days. If anyone accuses me of a crime, then I have to do penance. The accuser decides. But no one will accuse me,' she stated confidently. 'They all hated him. They are glad to see him dead.'

I said I was relieved to hear that, but it did not alter my basic situation, which was that I had to leave. I tried gently to detach myself from her embrace, but she clung to me more closely and with unexpected force. I would virtually have to wrestle with her to escape and I preferred to avoid that if possible. 'I'll stay for three days,' I compromised finally. 'Just to make sure you're all right. And then I must go. I have a wife and children in my homeland,' I lied.

She smiled. 'You will never leave,' she promised once again. 'You are one of us now.' She put her lips to mine in a long, sensuous kiss that left me shaken and breathless. 'And now we go to bed.' She took me by the hand and led me from the room, ignoring her dead husband and even brushing indifferently against his body as she passed, though I took care to skirt him and to avert my eyes.

'Tell me about Dr Daniels.'

I smile at the small, serious, six-year-old face beside me. He peers up at me intently, head tilted back, his eyes dark under the brim of his black hat. One day Ella will give me a son like that, one day he too will be a candidate for the Walking: he will seek advice from his elders, search diligently for wisdom. If he is successful, he will enter the Tower and learn the secrets of the Grotto. Two of the last batch of children, to the best of my knowledge, have not yet returned from their initiation; Ella tells me not to worry, they have been specially chosen to learn more than their fellows, or they are particularly dull and require additional teaching, she is not certain which. I think, however, of the black animal that leapt from the Institute's boat that evening, and I will not be content until I meet them on the street once again.

'Dr Daniels?' I describe him loping along the sand at midnight, under a full moon, snatching at unwary souls with his dripping jaws, gobbling them down. The child shudders in delicious ecstasy, his dark eyes widen as he waits for more. I explain the purpose of the nets and warn him of the dreadful consequences when the soul of a disobedient child, or of a foolish adult, attempts to evade the restrictions set up for its own benefit.

'For the time being, you are free,' I explain. 'Your soul can frolic happily with its friends, here or on the island. But when Dr Daniels returns . . .' I leave the warning mysterious, enigmatic.

'He will return?'

I give a sombre nod. He does not, I notice, say 'return', or even the garbled version of that word, and others like it, that the villagers often produce. What he says sounds nothing like their word for 'return' and yet I recognise it, I can understand what he means. And he, surprisingly, can follow my use of the traditional form of the words. I wonder how long this happy state of affairs will exist, before everything breaks into a babble of solipsistic miscomprehension. Perhaps this too is Daniels' doing, I muse, one of his tricks, one of his experiments.

To divert myself from these thoughts, I turn over one of the Seahorse cards before me. 'Now this,' I explain to him, 'is one of the most important of the cards. I call it *Old School Chums.*' My younger self stares at me solemnly from the card, from the centre of the group of black-suited children. The mangled body of a centipede lies at my feet, a stained clasp-knife is open in my fist. I tell him the card's value, its significance, its function in the total pattern of the game.

'And this one now.' I flip over the card named *Orgy*: the figures on the statue are frozen in the midst of frenzied and almost indecipherable activity, grappling together, intertwined. There are three or four human bodies there, one of them my own, and some kind of animal. I am shown mounting the animal, from the rear, but fortunately my face is turned away from the camera and one would have to know me intimately to recognise me.

I turn the card over hastily, without explanation. The statue cards change rapidly, I tell him, and by the time he is ready to play the game seriously, another image will have replaced this one. He gives a smile of understanding.

Hanslett enters the tavern, nods to me cordially, and takes a seat at his usual table. I signal to Ella to go and serve him. There was no point, we decided, once she returned unharmed from her three days at the crossroads, in continuing to keep the hotel open when we no longer had even one visitor. It would be better for her to serve in the tavern, saving us the expense of hiring a waitress, and to concentrate on cooking meals for the customers.

Lincott drifts in, with his usual group of friends. He too greets me amicably and they immediately set about a game of Seahorse. The fame of Ella's cooking has spread through the village already: we have more customers each day, more soon than we will be able to handle. I contemplate expansion already, division into a drinking area and one for eating, the acquisition of the neglected property next door, an ambitious scheme of decoration and renovation.

There is a dispute already at Lincott's table, a problem of interpretation, and I am called over to resolve it. I tell the boy that he can go and that I will talk to him again tomorrow. Before rising, I run my fingers through my thick, unkempt hair in an attempt to smooth it down. Ella tells me it is greyer and more distinguished each day, though I cannot, of course, check this in a mirror. Even pools of water and polished surfaces deny me my reflection, though I am convinced that yesterday there was a cloudy outline there, the merest hinting at a shape that, given time, might solidify and harden into something identifiable once more.

I walk heavily across to the table: Ella's cooking and lack of proper exercise have ballooned my figure to almost unrecognisable proportions already and I must impose some self-control soon before Maria and Martina return and find a further cause to scorn me. I expect I will still be here then, though I will move on shortly afterwards. A year here will be long enough and I do not wish to be seduced into total inertia by the undoubted comforts of my situation. I have much to do, in any case, and much to discover before I leave: I must recover my reflection fully; I must finish off the statue that now stands neglected on the headland, jutting a lopped-off and unfinished finger at the sky; I must visit and explore the grotto, which fills my dreams each night, its contents slithering into new and stranger alliances on each occasion, yet always with the promise of a clue that will unravel the tangle, reveal the hidden pattern; and I must – though I have never, for fear of ridicule, confessed this to anyone – row out to the rock where the mermaid suns herself each day, and try to question her.

I prop my hands on the edge of the table and lean forward. 'What seems to be the trouble, gentlemen?' Something catches in my throat and I wheeze unexpectedly, as if afflicted by asthma; I cough to clear it and smile round at them. The counters lie in a heap in the centre of the table, an indistinguishable mass of green and blue and all the possible shades and combinations between them; they remind me of the colours of the sea the day that Maria and Martina left, their boat dwindling to a barely visible dot on the turbulent waves. I give my verdict, which they all accept without question, and I linger for a moment more, watching the game. Daniels will surely bring them back with him, I assure myself, or, if not them, some other women who will provide a change from the monotony around me. Ella's eye catches mine as she brings in the first serving of the meal, a huge bowl of her speciality, her *bouillabaisse*; she smiles happily at me as moans of appreciation fill the air. Yes, Ella is the sort of woman who can satisfy me, in almost every way, for a few months, perhaps a year, but no longer than that. Maria is somehow closer to me, I can tell that, despite her outward mockery, and even Martina displayed moments of unexpected warmth. If I start off on the right footing with them next time, they will surely let me leave with them; meanwhile I loiter here, linger, filling in the months, and soon merely the weeks, until they return. . . .

Ella calls to me impatiently: my meal is ready. I lumber across the room and ease myself into my accustomed seat beside her. I lower my head almost to the level of the plate itself and inhale the fragrance that arises from the bowl. I sigh in genuine, unfeigned contentment. I begin to eat.